AF444951

AKUM

THE MAGIC OF DREAMS

GLORIA CHÁVEZ VÁSQUEZ

Cover Illustration: Angela Werneke copyright ©1996
Design: Lightbourne Images
Layout: Beloica Peña-Ruggiero

Copyright © Gloria Chávez Vásquez 2025
URL: http://www.gloriachavezvasquez.com

Goldeer Editions
3905 Tampa Road #5
Oldsmar, Fl., 34677
e-mail: goldeer.editions@gmail.com

ISBN: 979-8-9992305-2-2
Library of Congress Control Number: 2025944190

To **Clementina Hoyos Aguirre**
My beloved grandmother,
because her love is infinite

Author's Note

Originally, this story was written for a younger audience, but the warm reception of adult readers to the original Spanish edition broadened its readership. Bearing this in mind, *Akum: The Magic of Dreams* took on a more sophisticated, almost esoteric aspect in its expanded edition. Obviously, stories and philosophy evolved with history. Although the reading level requires a good knowledge of grammatical structure and vocabulary, the language is clear enough for readers of all ages to enjoy.

***Akum, The* Magic of dreams** was not written for those who close their minds to fantasy or to Yodin's books of knowledge. Instead, it is directed to all who respect life, have hope for the future, and are purposeful in contributing to a more compassionate world.

G.C.V.
May, 2025

Introduction

*"Life is a gift that must be returned
and joy must flow from its possession."*
Book of Infinite Sorrows

As an American son of Irish immigrants, I know what it means to grow up between two cultures: my own and that of my ancestors. The experience is not only fraught with conflicts, pain, and struggles, but also with challenges, knowledge, joys, and satisfactions. When I read *Akum: The Magic of Dreams,* I had the feeling that I was revisiting my youth. Through its protagonist, I relived my own dreams and fantasies. I had the opportunity to escape once again to that secret place of the mind, where I faced fears and anxieties as I moved through a new stage of life. In addition to the complete identification with each and every one of its characters, I came across characteristic figures quite familiar to me in my Irish culture: the goblins and the gnomes, which in Akum appear as universal archetypes rather than as particular elements of a specific national folklore.

Longtooth and *Chichigua,* the gnomes who appear in this story, are wandering beings who travel through the secret passages of the world, visiting children and good people to inspire them, not to kidnap them as tradition teaches. *Akum: The Magic of Dreams's* most precious revelation is a motto for the melting pot that is America: "The more different we are, the more we resemble each other."

I am sure that, as the reader, young or old, enters the wonderful world of this book, they will have the opportunity, as I did, not only to relive sorrows and joys but also to get closer to understanding, from the inside, a culture that has contributed to the world in so many ways.

With **Akum: The Magic of Dreams,** Gloria Chávez Vásquez has given us back the gift of life a hundred times, and her narrative reflects the pleasure of doing so

Welcome to the world of *Akum!*

Michael J. Crowley
New York

Prologue

There is in the general conception of *Akum: The Magic of Dreams* a fundamental, coherent vision of those submerged, dreamlike atmospheres, to which children give spontaneous adhesion. Within them, they achieve a gradual adjustment to the diffuse profiles of the apparent world.

In this climax of discoveries and deep subjectivisms, the singularity of the existence of Maribel, the protagonist, is defined: first as an adventure game, then as an experience whose sediments forge the being, and finally as knowledge, that dramatic process of uncertainty that places the human being in a social, cultural, and historical relativity.

This treatment of theme and characters is always preceded by the vital imprint of childhood, interwoven with dreams, terrors, and dazzles, an expression of a sociocultural environment, rich in contrasts, contradictions, and passion.

And all this is because of the powers of children, which makes them participants in the inventions of nature, which gives them something in its mysterious signs, its keys, not yet desecrated, and its metamorphosis.

Rigor and creative flight allow the reader to

access that dimension of childhood, that threshold of the marvelous that represents the initiatory steps. That is, the transit of mythical splendors, what begins to be named, assumed to the extent that it is deciphered and incorporated, between a conscious or unconscious choice, into the realm of the avid self: the center of high alchemies, becoming the fruit of individuality and social being.

Here is a rough outline of a highly imaginative temperature feature, backed up without a doubt by a solid intellectual formation, but, above all, by an incredible authenticity. This is what this lively and vigorous story by **Gloria Chávez Vásquez** reveals.

It is known that the literary treatment of the materials that make up the varied and fascinating universe of children entails technical difficulties that are not easy to overcome. However, our author resolves them with singular skill in the use of the language, and an inventive audacity that ends up recreating the atmosphere with a geographical, human, cultural, and historical content where childhood memories, dreams, legends, and superstitions merge into an organic whole, with a procession of elves and apparitions. That is to say, a vision of deep telluric content, with a folk background, where play is mixed with drama, sarcasm with humor, reality with dream, and where a longing for justice and a tormented effort to define the identity of a world persists. An exquisite synthesis of the anthropological sign, elevated to a great aesthetic dignity.

Maribel is the character with whom the author condenses, with extraordinary literary sagacity, the elements of childhood. The author manages to transport the reader to the realm of the marvelous real, in the midst of a homely environment, and in whose objects the memories of past generations are trapped. These manifestations try to condition the behavior patterns of the younger generations, all of them confused with their respective generations of goblins, gnomes, and legendary creatures that, in the childhood of humanity, represent the spirit of natural forces.

In one of the moments of unease, the young heroine, annoyed more by the waves of her imagination than by what she calls the incomprehension of adults, begins contact with these intimate secrets of nature through the reading of a book of stories. And the adventure begins: reality reverts into a kind of magic, and the girl's dialogue with the ineffable is established.

In the course of the narrative, the writer manages to create a diaphanous climate where everything is natural, complete. The world of dreams, real, and imagined characters are confused without artifice because deep down, the girl, Maribel, has begun to understand that the profound meaning of life lies in the capacity of the human being to integrate himself into the contradictory unity and diversity of nature.

Finally, we will highlight three aspects that define Gloria Chávez Vásquez's qualities as a writer:

First, the balance of her language, which she establishes by virtue of a transparent verbal movement rich in poetic findings. Its vision is as a communicating vehicle and an instrument of an expressive individuality, because the word exercises its mission of revealing underlying essences on the underside of reality and the interactions between culture, environment, and social dynamics.

Second, the well-articulated organic conception of the story in which the children's universe is recreated. The writer does not omit any of the essential features of the particular that is realized in the universal: filial feelings, vernacular gifts, the encounter with solidarity and companionship, love, and procreation. All this is interwoven with vicissitudes in the course of which the imagination opens up to the vertiginous movement of a reality, which, by itself, has the genetic power to shape behavior, while at the same time being a transmitter of the vital load sustained by magical vision and playful splendor.

And third, the perfect warp that constitutes the lively gallery of characters, real and imaginary, arising from ancestral and personal memory, and which are integrated into an organic whole. The children's world, the circle of grandparents, parents, cousins, uncles, siblings, nature, and flowers, plants, fruits, animals, water, and minerals are concentrated in space and time, in a highly humanized environment that the author masterfully captures with her clean handling of literary technique.

The tools of the trade are used in *Akum* without rhetorical artifice. The result is a clean and magnificent design, in chiaroscuro and light, of the eternal landscape of the children's soul.

Jorge Vélez
Anthropologist and writer
Author of *The Jason of the Andes*
Bogota, Colombia

I

The House Game

If we gave food, joy, and songs more value than gold,
this would certainly be a happier world.

— J.R.R. Tolkien

"Mama says that if we behave, she'll allow us to spend the night in the playhouse," the girl announced to her siblings. She placed the provisions for the cookout in the improvised kitchen she and her younger brother and sister had set up in the patio that morning.

Maribel thought Miriam's message sounded too good to be true. Was she speaking of the very same mother who had threatened to knock down their shack if they kept coming into the house with muddy feet?

But the plantain, the yucca, the potato, and even the jug of milk, which her sister could barely carry, somehow confirmed that their mother had finally accepted the idea that the children were entitled to their stick house.

Papito didn't even bother to look up, occupied as he was in inspecting his firetruck. He examined it in the same puzzled way Maribel looked at things when she was his age. She could tell he was still reluctant to play the father's role, under the excuse that he was still too young; therefore, he could only play the baby. He demanded that his sisters serve him quickly because he was mighty hungry.

"Mamita says, 'He who doesn't work doesn't eat!'" Maribel protested, quoting her grandmother and adding that it would be wise for him to help toss the twigs into the fire so that they could start frying the plantain slices.

"You don't know how to cook!" the boy sneered.

"Then don't come asking for our food!" Miriam replied.

The girls had just begun to wash the vegetables when they heard their mother's annoyed voice from above: "Who's been taking the vegetables from my kitchen!" And then she proceeded to yell: "Maribel!"

"You said Mom gave us permission!" She looked at her sister, doubt showing on her face.

"They were ready, on the table! I thought she had prepared everything for us to pick up!" Miriam responded.

"What did she say about allowing us to sleep in the little house?"

"Well, I thought that maybe... she wouldn't mind if..."

"Maribel, come up immediately!" Her mother shouted once more.

"Now look at the trouble you have gotten me into!" Maribel frowned at her sister.

Reluctantly, she collected the booty Miriam had brought "by mistake."

II

The Universe of the House

*There are feelings that cannot be given verbal body,
but it is possible to follow perfectly with your eyes closed.*

— **Horacio Quiroga**

Maribel had discovered this rule a day before school opened, and she officially became a third grader: *Mothers didn't want you to write on the family albums.* The painful discovery was related to her interest in solving the perpetual house mysteries, whose exploration fascinated her.

Three chests were as valuable as treasures to the family. One belonged to Mamita; the second one was her mother's. But there was a third one that attracted her the most. The old wooden one, of antique design, fastened with rusty nails, reinforced with iron blades, reminiscent of barrels, belonged to Aunt Marina. Always open, always in inventory status. Aunt Marina sitting by its side or on the floor, surrounded by an aura of curiosity of the children, revealing the magic of music and poetry. An accordion, a harmonica, and their own whistles intoning the "tiobín tiobán" with the rhythm taught by *la tia*, Maribel, trying to decipher the notes drawn in the music notebooks, like black swallows perched on telephone wires.

A kaleidoscope, the gift from Uncle Louis to his niece, fed sight and imagination with geometric shapes. A simple but marvelous tube projected a world of colorful patterns, seen, as if they were pirates, with only one eye at a time. The black and white glossy portraits of actors and actresses of the Mexican cinema, collected by Marina, and which came wrapped in candies, were already arranged and pasted on the pages of an album, not as serious as the family's, but so special to her.

The blue ink, the German stylograph, priceless objects with which Aunt Marina and Uncle Alberto wrote or copied poetry during their courtship and then read them to each other as the romantic declaration of their love. Aunt Marina's trunk had been locked on the day of her marriage, but it remained at the grandmother's house, so she could revisit her bachelorette's world.

The lightly burnished wooden one, scented of perfume, belonged to the mother and was rarely opened, so that its opening was always an event. Then the colorful possessions came to light, preceded by the fragrances, cologne, soaps, incense, and talc penetrating the fibers of the fabrics, the silk scarves, and the jewels of dubious value that sparkled in the children's eyes. The family albums, a privilege of visits or moments of leisure shared with the young ones, meant the challenge of being able to identify the sepia-colored figures whose sorrows and glories only existed in the memory of the grandmother. Older people were illustrated in black and white portraits. The younger ones were already depicted in the colored photos.

Grandma's inner world was not confined to her trunk. It encompassed her entire house, converted into a greenhouse, an antiquarian, and a zoo in the name of *Micifú*, the Angora cat, and *Lolita* the parrot, as much part of the family as the plants of infinite variety. The ancient table, the old Singer sewing machine, the wooden native sculptures, the RCA Victrola, which struggled to prolong its musical sounds, and the charcoal iron, replaced by the electric one, of her arduous tasks. All this and more formed part of Mamita's personal Time Museum.

***

Fearing that her family, in time, would be forgotten, Maribel had applied herself to writing the names and relationships on each photo in the family albums. The dumb initiative had so angered her mother that the girl had finally earned the much-feared blow on the head. Delivered with the fist and the knuckle of the middle finger sticking out like a human beak, it caused the equivalent of a lightning sent by God to expel her from paradise. "I just wanted to do the family a favor!" She had protested with tears of indignation. Her mother had refused her explanation.

"So that people don't forget about us!" Maribel said to herself.

"And who is thinking of dying yet?" The mother reproached her blasphemy.

Didn't our ancestors die? And no one at home knew the name of that skinny and frightened girl who appeared in the photos with the uncles. Or whose daughter she was, or how old. They didn't even know if she was alive! Who had that girl been? Herminia herself wondered.

"Some nosy girl, just like you!" She pointed out, understanding, deep down, her daughter's anxieties.

"I won't do any favors anymore!" Maribel announced before leaving the room. Her mother looked back at her as if she were telling a joke.

"Go scribble in your notebooks!" Herminia snapped at her daughter as she began the task of repairing the albums.

***

Maribel took refuge in the living room. She sat on the floor behind the sofa, placed in front of the large bookcase. There she cried for a while about the lack of understanding of the elders, until she became tired and ran out of tears. She fell asleep for a while and then woke up disoriented.

She had to think twice to remember where she was. She decided to stay longer in her hiding place to teach her mother a lesson. When she realized that her daughter had disappeared, Herminia would regret how unfair she had been.

And that's when she noticed the position of the bookshelf. Placed diagonally against the wall, the furniture left a free space. As best she could, she slipped through the small crack left by the wall and bookshelf. As she had seen Micifú do many times, she compressed her body by holding her breath. Stretched, as if made of rubber, she was quickly on the other side. The space was neither large nor small, but it fit perfectly when she curled up.

Now she could wait as long as it took for someone to report her missing. Perhaps Miriam would come in search of her, looking to play a game. Possibly her little brother, Papito, with whom she preferred to adventure, was already asking about her. Ah, and soon the bottle of warm milk would have to be given to little Lucy, her youngest sister.

She was sure that her mother would call her for homework. It wouldn't be long before anyone became curious about her whereabouts. Or simply Mamita, going through the list of her grandchildren to find out who was missing, would finally ask: "Where is Maribel?"

And even if she didn't care, her mom would have to look for her to give Mamita an answer. If all this failed, there was one last chance, when her father, returning from work, sat in the dining room, waiting for his meal, noticed, counting the heads, that something wasn't right, and curiously asked: "Who is missing here?"

The wait could be extended, and an hour became eternal when a girl was hiding. She had already lost interest, and there was nothing and no one to play with in that corner of her world. Not even ants, as would have been the case if she had gone to hide in the yard. But she would have gotten herself into a real mess and would have risked staying out all night.

How long did it take for her mother to repent?

III

The Dimension of Books

*I always imagined that Paradise would be
some kind of library.*

— **Jorge Luis Borges**

*I*t was getting dark, and Maribel was feeling bored. She would go out for a moment. She would scout her parents' bedroom and return immediately to her hiding place. She could hear nothing but her heartbeat.

There were no Moors on the coast, so she slipped through the crack she had first entered. The girl went straight to the bedside table where her mother invariably kept a couple of candles and matches, just in case. Being upset and crying had awakened her appetite. Mealtime seemed so far away, but she decided that in protest for the mistreatment, she was not going to eat dinner.

She would not eat until they begged her, please, to eat. Otherwise, she was going to starve to death, and they couldn't live without her. Or, as it could happen, one of her siblings would take pity and, secretly, would bring her a bite. That way, she would not run the risk of starving.

Herminia had crossed the door that connected their house with Mamita's to chat and have their *algo* of hot chocolate with *buñuelos*. Maribel heard the voices of Papito, Miriam, and little Lucy playing with other children in the neighborhood. They seemed to be having a lot of fun, but she was glad to be alone.

Quietly, she tiptoed to the kitchen and placed a chair so that she could reach the tin of crackers that were on a shelf of the cupboard. Grabbing a handful, she pocketed them on her apron. Then, she opened the tin of powdered milk, emptied several teaspoons into a mug, and added sugar. After stirring the compound, she put everything back in its place and returned to her hiding place.

Now she could spend a whole week in her hideaway with these provisions, if she didn't have to go back to school tomorrow, that is.

Maribel reached the bookcase, picked out a couple of books from the *Treasure of Youth* encyclopedia, slid them along with the mug, and then curled up on the floor. Placing the provisions on a napkin and lighting one of the candles, she opened one of the books and flipped through it. She stopped at the beautiful illustration of the little girl sitting in a field of flowers, in the same position she was now. A little poem engraved in the clouds caught her attention: "The world was mine, in it I reigned…"

The girl continued reading and enjoying the illustrations until she reached the story of the wandering gnomes who traveled underground. She was amused by the two creatures in the drawing. They had old faces, childish bodies, and wore the colors of the earth. They were camouflaged by the flowers and the bushes. The eldest carried a kind of leather bag. Both wore some sort of espadrilles, and their clothes were simple and full of patches. Lore told of tiny houses they built in big mushrooms. She had never seen one!

The old man with the long, sparse white beard seemed to scold the younger, a beardless little gnome, with abundant hair, short but tousled. Judging by his knapsack, hanging from a rod and leaning on his right shoulder, they were about to set out on a journey.

"Beware of humans! They think they own us! They are forever on the lookout to trap us, to enslave us, and force us to do things for them. That's disgraceful to a gnome!" the old man warned the young one.

Maribel raised the candle so she could see better.

"Who's there?" The old gnome shrieked in alarm as the little one ran, hiding behind a rock.

"Nobody, nobody!" Maribel replied, more

frightened than they already were.

"If you're nobody, then why do you speak?" yelled the gnome impatiently and exclaiming: "Darnation!"

Squinting his eyes, the young one exclaimed from the other side of the rock: "It looks like a human child, master!"

"How the hell did you get here?" asked the annoyed old gnome while approaching the girl.

"I don't know! I was merely reading...!" Maribel was confused. She was trying to explain what had happened to her. She felt a lump of excitement, surprise, fear, and above all, curiosity, in her throat. Not knowing how, she was part of the drawing on the page of the book.

"What do you have there?" The little old man pointed suspiciously at the mug Maribel was holding in her hands.

"Nothing!" she said, weighing the object in her left hand. Reconsidering, she answered timidly: "A candle... and a mug!"

"What's that white thing?" The gnome said, questioning the powder, ready to find out on his own.

"Don't touch!" said the girl. "It's powdered milk!"

"Milk? That? Whose milk?" The grumpy gnome made Maribel nervous and angry.

"Milk for people! For babies! Mainly." She explained.

"I'm sure you're trying to trick us with a magic powder!" The gnome sounded irritated but acted with precaution.

"No, no, no! I promise!" Said Maribel, carefully sticking the candle on top of the rock and offering the mug for him to examine.

"Don't you dare!" he warned his young companion, who had finally come out of his hiding place behind the rock.

"It's just milk with sugar from Mom's kitchen," she said and remembered: "She must be worried about me already!" Maribel looked at the little gnome who was watching her more sympathetically.

"Do you have a good mother?" he asked tenderly.

"Yes!" she replied, smiling at the friendly gnome.

"It's that cow's milk by any chance?" The grumpy one sniffed. Maribel ignored his question.

"And, surely you must have family and friends?" speculated the little one.

"Of course!" retorted the old gnome, "and they will all soon come after us. Go away, go away, go away!" he shouted to the girl, jumping and stomping like a maniac.

"I've already told you that I came here by accident!" The girl said.

"Liar! You want us to believe you fell out of thin air, out of nowhere?"

"Don't call me that, you rude old man!" Maribel

was about to cry when the little gnome suggested:

"We can help her get back home if she's lost, Master Longtooth."

"She would have to pay us and promise that she won't deceive us!" added the so-called Longtooth, a nickname curiously appropriate for the single tooth that protruded from his mouth the few times he had it shut.

"I don't have any money," said the girl, placing the mug on the rock to check her pockets and noticing that what was left of the crackers had been pulverized.

"But you have other valuable things that we can accept. That milk, for example. I mean, if it's really milk and not a poisonous substance," the old man pointed at the compound from a distance.

The girl didn't bother to give further explanations to the gnome. It was like defending herself before obnoxious adults. She had grown tired of tolerating the arrogant gnome and was making little progress in convincing him that she was telling the truth. It was easier to communicate with the little one.

"What's your name?" She asked him.

"Olaf, but around here they know me as Chichigua. You can call me Chichi."

Maribel had to restrain herself from laughing. Chichigua was the nickname given to first-grade students. "I was called that once myself," she explained to the young gnome so that he would not be offended.

"I am Maribel, and can you please find out what place this is and what we are doing here?"

"We are *guaqueros* looking for the gold that the indigenous people of these regions buried in ceramic pots all over the land," Chichigua replied.

"Ah! You are looking for burials or *guacas*!" She exclaimed, remembering the stories her mother had told her. Whoever found a guaca would become rich beyond measure. It was necessary to overcome the panic of *fuego fatuo* or will-o'-the-wisps, the ghosts that guarded the treasures, until they were discovered by a lucky person.

"Mama says there's possibly a *guaca* in our backyard."

The old man was skeptical but still asked, "And if it is true, how is it that you haven't dug it up?"

"Because the indigenous spirits guard the burials. Sometimes, terrible misfortunes befall people who discover them. Besides, it would have to be dug up at night, and we don't dare," she said.

"They will do nothing to us," bragged Longtooth. "That gold has been ours since the beginning of time."

"Do you want a little bit?" Maribel offered Chichigua some powdered milk.

"Truly? You are going to share with us?" Chichi sounded delighted.

"First, I have to show you how to taste it," and, moistening her index finger with her tongue, she plunged it right into the powder. She licked the powder adhering to her finger with delight. The gesture sparked the appetite of the gnomes.

"The last time we tasted it, the cow got so scared that the milk soured in its udder," Chichi recalled.

"Is it really cow's milk?" The old man was doubtful.

"And how does it turn into dust?" Chichi asked.

"It is a secret formula," she was sure.

"What are you saying, silly girl? Do you think there are secrets that we gnomes don't know?"

"You don't know where the *guacas* are buried, do you?" Maribel said as Chichi plunged his finger into the white dust.

Longtooth's rage turned to nostalgia as soon as he tasted the sweet powdered milk, and as if he had realized the futility of fighting with the girl. Talking to himself, carefully pronouncing his words, he went to sit on the rock.

"Our cousins from Atlantis were rather careless. We, the natives of Lemuria, used to tell them: 'Don't be so generous with people; you will make them take advantage of you. Do not share secrets or deal with evil humans.' But it was to no avail. Then our relatives in the medieval villages became passionate about alchemy, a dangerous game invented by treacherous men to subjugate nature. Ulman, a wise gnome, warned them about exchanging secrets for stupid trinkets. Many of our brothers fell into the trap, attracted by the containers of cream of milk that sneaky humans placed in their doorways to hunt them down and make them their servants."

Longtooth's eyes paused on the ground for a while, then unexpectedly seemed to focus on reality. As if his previous words had been a parenthesis to his bad temper, he resumed the scolding of his pupil: "I repeat for the millionth time, Olaf, be wary of humans. Sharing our secrets means extinction."

"But this is a little girl! And not every human is evil!"

"You don't know for certain! No matter how small, they're harmful!" he said, giving the girl a strange glance to conclude: "She's but a fool!"

"Stop insulting me!" Maribel protested. "I wouldn't make any deals with you either. Adults say worse things about you people!"

"Oh, yes? What do they say?"

"To begin with, that you abduct children," Maribel replied.

"What? That is a very serious accusation! We don't steal children; they choose to come with us."

"Tell that to any mother."

"What else do they say about us?" Chichi was intrigued.

"That you are creatures of the devil." The two gnomes burst out laughing.

"Do you believe that nonsense?" Tooth asked.

"Well, my dad says you don't exist, except in fairy tales. He believes that there is no one in the world with such powers."

"Oh, no? Let you meet Akum!" offered Chichi.

"Shut up, you useless dwarf! And you! Forget that name at once. Akum is not interested in meeting ignorant people."

"Oh, yes? But he has met you, hasn't he?" Maribel rebutted.

Longtooth was about to let out one of his curses when Chichigua stepped forward:

"We haven't seen him in person. Agmmandiel is the only one who can."

"If you keep talking," Tooth said, threatening Chichi with his fist, "I'm going to hit you in that big mouth of yours, and you won't be able to speak for months, you hear?" Tooth's face was turning purple, while Chichi was on the verge of tears. Yet he spoke. "That's no secret, Master Tooth. Agmmandiel is known to all the creatures of the forest. Although he is cunning, if he is your friend, he won't deceive you."

"Well," Tooth reconsidered. He allowed a wicked smile on his face, "only if we lead her to him ourselves. But don't blame me afterwards."

"What am I going to blame you for?" inquired Maribel.

"Agmmandiel is a rascal... but, on second thoughts, you deserve to meet him."

"Do we need a candle? It's pretty dark!" She asked, mostly worried about the growing breeze that threatened to extinguish the flame.

"Silly! In the dark, you can see with your ears!"

IV

The Treasure Hunters

Six honest servants taught me all I know.
Their names are how, when, where, what, who and why.

— **Rudyard Kipling**

*T*hey went deep into the forest. Each tree, each plant, each flower seemed to Maribel to be part of the most exotic vegetation of the jungle, contained only in the book of unknown species.

The faint light of the candle scarcely competed with the moonlight, but it had the power to reveal at times the figures of the nocturnal birds, creatures of colors invisible to the human eye, hidden in the charm of the night. The animals of the forest rested in their shelters, in their damp hollows, or in their warm nests. The moving creatures struck like lightning on the path. Others, more cautious, camouflaged themselves in the thicket. The noises were an impressive addition to the equally gloomy visions. Maribel regretted having been so curious.

"We'd better go back," she whispered to the gnomes, "it's late and tomorrow is the first day of school. We'll be back another day."

The gnomes paid no attention to the girl, but when the birds heard her voice, they burst into a melody of mysterious notes. There was no sign that their journey would end anytime soon. One sound in particular made her startle.

Sheesheetah! The echo of that kind of human whisper filled the forest.

"It's the cricket, you fool!" Longtooth groaned. The old man, who did not stop grumbling, began an interesting story that managed to divert the girl's attention from the dark specter of the night.

"Many, many years ago, we gnomes could go wherever we wanted. There were passages all over the world. Well, almost everywhere. Some folks closed them to us. Over time, more and more were sealed. And people forgot about us. Still, we continued building routes. The ancient paths were so beautiful that many respectable creatures gladly shared in our adventures. Eventually, and as human societies became more complicated, we ourselves sealed the entrances and exits to protect ourselves and our secrets. We lost communication with our cousins in those regions where we used to travel directly, in less time than it takes to tell this story. Even so, we managed to survive. But there are other reasons why people can't see us anymore," Tooth concluded.

"Poor things!" said the girl.

"Don't pity us! We are still guardians of Nature. And we are always cautious when sharing its secrets with the wise. Others lost their common sense, and it seems to me that they have become such pitiful beings that they no longer have a reason to live."

"And why don't you open new entries?"

"It's not easy," Chi replied.

"The trouble began," Longtooth went on, "when the three books of Yodin were stolen. On them were written the keys to the seven powers."

"Who is Yodin?" Maribel was intrigued.

"The Wise Keeper of the Books of Knowledge, one of the Masters of the Fellowship," Tooth informed her with a relish that surprised the girl.

"Fellowship?" The word itself sounded mysterious.

"The Fellowship of the White Feather, a lodge made up of magicians, sorcerers, and very special people," Tooth replied.

"And who stole the books?" she asked.

"One of his apprentices. They say that he stole them to give them to a very ambitious man, who planned to conquer the world and who promised to share his power with the thief."

"And then what happened?"

"They betrayed each other!" replied the gnome.

"It is written in Yodin's books: Evil destroys itself," Chi quoted, proud to know the lesson.

"And now, where are those books?"

"Two of them were recovered with the help of Akum, a warrior prince of the Chibcha race, whom, in gratitude, Yodin appointed Main Guardian of these lands. But the third one still needs to be recovered. Yodin has not entrusted the custody of the books to anyone, ever since. Whenever there are catastrophes like these, we have to start by undoing the stupidities committed during the madness that power engenders. But I have already said too much."

"She'll soon forget everything, Master," it occurred to Chi.

"I don't forget anything!" The girl announced, provoking a look of complicity between the two gnomes.

"What is Agmmandiel like?" Maribel asked when the gnomes stepped into the clearing surrounded by a circle of trees.

"You'll know when he appears," said Tooth, demanding silence with a gesture. Then, with great drama, he examined the terrain. Listening intently, he cleared his throat and stomped three times with his right foot. A high-pitched whistle seemingly came from a strange bird. A gust blew out the candle, but fortunately, the moonlight prevailed.

As if responding to the ritual, a whirlwind emanated from the ground surrounding the trio. For some unknown reason, the dust produced by the whirlwind began to glow like a shower of tiny stars. A mysterious energy surrounded them. A silent explosion, green and blue, generated a beautiful bird with long feathers, broad wings, and a silver and gold crest. On its tail were the colors of the rainbow. The bird ascended as fast as the phenomenon that had produced it. When the lights faded, leaving only the lunar blue, the bird descended at great speed while initiating a fantastic transformation.

The bird had transformed into an indigenous boy of exceptional beauty. His hair, the bluish-black color of the raven, was covered with a crown of tiny white flowers. A lace of colored beads hung from his neck. He was wearing a loincloth and espadrilles finely woven with hemp fiber. At one point, the boy, who seemed to levitate, jumped onto a branch where he paused with unknown intentions.

"Greetings, little brothers of the forest!" he giggled. His large amber-colored eyes sparkled like fireflies. Maribel couldn't decide whether the boy was a native, a spirit, an angel, or all of that when the creature sang a song that invited reverie:

I bring gold in both my hands
And to metal I give shape
I'm the spirit of the tree
I'm the soul of truest love
I am guardian of the children

> *I'm the one that'll always be*
> *Agmmandiel cares for the roses*
> *Agmmandiel nourishes the sage*
> *Agmmandiel serves the wild kingdom*
> *And yet, no one can see him!*

"Except us, you rascal!" Longtooth exclaimed, crossing the fingers of both his hands as if by the gesture he was assuring the boy's presence.

"Release me, you witch dwarf!" Agmmandiel yelled in pain, covering his ears.

"Let go of him, *Señor* Tooth!" begged Maribel, while the old gnome now controlled with his eyes the movements of the boy, no bigger in stature than the girl.

"It's time you gave us the answer to your silly riddle! We need to see Akum urgently!" Tooth demanded.

"The answer to the riddle is the key to the mountain of Akum," Chichi explained to Maribel.

"I can hardly remember the verses, much less guess at their meaning," she said.

"He refuses to reveal it!" said Chichi, looking at the boy.

"Promise you'll give us a clue," Tooth demanded with a short-tempered look. "And don't play one of your tricks on us."

"Yes, I promise, I promise, but let me go!" exclaimed the elf.

When Tooth uncrossed his fingers, Agmmandiel heaved a sigh of relief. But at once, he sat up angrily:

"What are you looking for, old crook?"

"The *guacas* you hide from us!"

"Ask the one who still has Yodin's book!"

"We have nothing to do with the matter..."

"But your foolishness makes you vulnerable to evil..."

Longtooth was about to renew the torture when Maribel intervened.

"No more, please! Do you like being forced to do what you don't want to do?"

"Who is this little girl and what is she doing here?" Agmmandiel was curious.

"She wants to meet Akum," Tooth informed him wryly.

"Impossible," said Agmmandiel, "if she can see us, it's because she has some talent, but first, we must find out what it is."

Agmmandiel produced a twig in the shape of a pitchfork, which first appeared suspended in the air and then fell at Chichigua's feet.

"This is better than a map, little brother. By the time the enchantment ends, you'll be an expert finder of indigenous burials. Follow your instinct. But if you break the rules, you'll never find *guacas* in these lands."

"Thank you, thank you very much!" Chi exclaimed, picking up the twig.

"And why do you want to see Akum?" Agmmandiel turned his attention to Maribel as he floated up and down the tree.

"She's looking for magical powers," Tooth told him.

Agmmandiel laughed all the way to the ground. When he landed next to Maribel, he looked her in the eye and said very seriously, "No one has access to those powers anymore. Not even the elves. And Yodin has sentenced us: the next time we give power to a human being, we'll be condemned to serve the stones."

"I don't want powers or magical objects," Maribel protested, "I don't want to get you in trouble or anything like that. I only want to be able to do things well and for adults to understand me once and for all."

"Maybe it would be easier for you to understand people," the elf suggested.

"But it seems that there are very few fair or just people. Only in fairy tales!" Maribel concluded.

"Not true!" Agmmandiel exclaimed, seconded by the gnomes. "What you need is to learn the difference between good and evil. Didn't your elders teach you that?" He asked curiously. "Or, perhaps what you are looking for is wisdom," the elf concluded with a confident smile, "In which case, it's possible you have the talent Akum looks for in humans."

To add to Maribel's confusion, Longtooth came up with his usual harshness: "But first you have to solve the enigma."

"What enigma?" She asked, discouraged.

"Agmmandiel's riddle!" Chichi said, as if it were public knowledge.

Agmmandiel recited his poem to refresh her memory.

"But what does it mean? What am I supposed to say?" questioned Maribel.

"A simple word! The word that started all this nonsense!" replied Tooth, sharing the girl's frustration.

"A word? And, if I guess it, will I be able to see Akum?" She hoped.

"When you come up with it, you must say it in front of The Bridge of Illusions," Agmmandiel said.

"The bridge of what?"

"The bridge that leads to Akum Mountain, of course!" the little gnome was amused.

That sounded like the greatest adventure, and nothing she could do without her parents' permission.

"I'd like to be your guide," the boy offered. "Akum needs the help of special humans." Maribel didn't know if he was joking or being serious.

"This rascal is always up to something," Tooth warned her.

Maribel felt she could trust him. Still, she didn't know what to think. Her first question was, "How many letters did the magic word have? Would it be as easy to find it as in *the hanged man?*" She mastered that game already. Or would it have the logic of riddles?

She was intrigued by Agmmandiel's hypnotic eyes. They reminded her, inevitably, of Micifú's grandmother's angora cat. And weren't those in his crown the same flowers that Mamita had planted in her garden? And, had she not dreamed of those splendid feathers when he became a celestial bird?

"Girl! We have to leave before the roosters crow," Tooth announced hurriedly.

When she was about to ask him for a little clue about the mysterious word, it was too late. Agmmandiel disappeared before her very eyes. She still could see the silhouette of the elf boy among the leaves and the trunks of the trees. A squirrel jumped from the same spot he had previously occupied. Maribel turned to look for the gnomes, but they had also vanished.

She was all alone, there, in the middle of the forest. There were no more noises or strange sounds. At that moment, a rooster crowed.

"Wait for me, Chichi, Tooth!" She called with no results. She wanted to let them know that there was no secret to the powdered milk, but that she could take it from the tin jar in the kitchen whenever she wanted. She felt better when she discovered that they had taken the mugful of milk.

She only wished on returning with the light of dawn.

The sun's rays happily entered the house, announcing the first day of school. Maribel woke up in her bed, trying in vain to remember her dream.

"I BRING GOLD IN BOTH MY HANDS
AND TO METAL I GIVE SHAPE
I'M THE SPIRIT OF THE TREE
I'M THE SOUL OF TRUEST LOVE"

V

The Enigma of Agmmandiel

Integrity is doing the right thing, even if no one is watching.
— C. S. Lewis

"Ma, I don't want to use the pencil and eraser as a necklace anymore!" Maribel protested. She was no longer a little girl! In addition, her classmates would make fun of her.

While she buttoned their white uniforms, Herminia reminded her daughters they should bring the list of books so that their father could go to the stationery store to buy everything they needed so that they could start their readings and homework as soon as possible.

"I'm sure they're going to ask us for ink and a pen," Maribel figured, because that had been the case with Amanda's sister, the one who had graduated last year. Now she knew what it was like to reach that stage. The Boyacá school only had up to the third grade. After that, you had to continue the fourth and fifth at one of the public schools in the center of the small city.

"And they're going to ask us for maps and colors, I'm sure," Miriam said excitedly, mentioning some of her favorite items.

Enthusiastically, and while the girls were having breakfast, they discussed their school prospects. They had not finished the *arepa* with cheese and butter when they heard a great commotion coming from their brother's bed. Rigoberto and Herminia took turns waking up the child to bring him to the bathroom.

Papito didn't seem very happy with the idea of having to go to school for the first time. His sisters, including three-year-old Lucy, couldn't explain the terror he was experiencing just to prepare for the most important journey: learning and giving a purpose to one's life.

Papito cried inconsolably as he left the house. "You'll see that you're going to like school," his father assured him, but the boy's panic did not let up. It seemed to him that he was leaving for good.

"I wish we could help him," Maribel sighed as she prompted Miriam to hurry up because the school's bell was about to peal. The little sisters were getting ready to cross the street when Maribel noticed the neat and handsome boy, perkily walking while carrying a briefcase with his left hand and nibbling a *pandebono* with his right. The boy reminded her of someone. But who?

"He's going to the Franciscan school," she assured her sister.

"How do you know?" Miriam asked.

"Because he's dressed in a collar and tie," Maribel said.

A thought assailed her before entering the school. It had to do with a certain mysterious word that she was supposed to find.

***

Maribel still savored the fact that she had been a good student in first grade. How proud she had been when Doña Lola had set her as an example for being the first student to learn to read and write! And the first to know the tables and to recite without failing the poems and the answers to the catechism!

Best of all, she had been commissioned by the teacher to recite the poetry of Rafael Pombo, Amado Nervo, and Gabriela Mistral during school presentations. What did all her anxiety matter now, although it still made her lose her voice and forget her lines!

However, things at school hadn't always been perfect. Maribel hadn't exactly been the best student in second grade. But she didn't feel totally responsible. No sooner had she become accustomed to the first teacher than at least three others had passed through her course in a single school year.

The teachers seemed slow to start and, in a hurry, to leave, as if they didn't like the school, the students, or the principal. In the final exams, the examining master had been so impatient with her that Maribel had become a nervous wreck, and she hadn't been able to decide where an "acute" word was accented.

After the scare of the oral exam, the humiliation (in front of his mother!) had made her realize (too late!) that the most natural place to pronounce the accent on the word *perro* was on the first syllable. She had given the wrong answer, not because she didn't know, but because she wanted to prove to the teacher that she wasn't a slow student. To top it off, the woman's comment to her mother had been:

"I don't know how this girl has such high grades!"

Her mother had come to her defense, replying: "I don't think, as a teacher, you'd do any better!"

Vacation time had hardly made her forget the awful moment. But she had confirmed then that many discoveries could be made without going very far or even having an adult follow her steps to approve the results.

If she had been asked to write a composition about her vacation, she would have had to say that she had not gone anywhere. Although perhaps she could talk about the little house of sticks. Or about her readings. Maybe the new teacher would like to hear what her mom had taught her that summer: plants had a language and feelings of their own, just like people!

One discovery she would never talk about would be about her most recent, precious secret: her adventure, or was it a dream, in the hiding place behind the bookshelf of her house. Her most solemn resolution for this school year was to explore the wonderful world of books.

***

Maribel recognized most of the students who were beginning to line up next to the school's garden. The place was reserved for third-grade students. Not only would they be closer to enjoy and smell the flowers, because they were the oldest in school, but they would even be the envy of the *chichiguas.*

Chichigua, what was in the word that brought her images of forests, jungles, gnomes, elves, and birds? It had to do with her dream from the night before. If only she could remember it!

The crop of this year's third graders would prepare to ride a bus to the fourth grade in a school up north. The thought of traveling was exciting. She had to apply so as not to be left behind.

"Adalgiza! Nelly!" She saw her friends arrive, followed by Mariela and Amanda. They lined up together while waiting for the second peal of the bell that would prompt the alumnae to keep absolute silence. Meanwhile, the small group bent the line in a semicircle so they could talk about their vacation. It was a totally new experience for the girls.

Nothing like this happened in the first grade. They all seemed so busy learning to read and write, multiply and divide, trying not to break the rules. But having reached the third grade had given the group confidence and a feeling of sisterhood. It was something akin to love, a feeling different from what was felt for family members or from the brief emotions felt for people. It was such an extraordinary feeling of belonging that she wouldn't have wanted to miss it for anything in the world.

"Does anyone know what room we are going to be in?" Amanda's question prompted her classmates to study the four possible alternatives in the small colonial-style building. The room regularly used for third-grade classes remained closed.

"Maybe they'll give us the second classroom," guessed Adalgiza, the freckled, red-haired girl.

"Something extraordinary is going on," Maribel concluded when observing the teachers talking among each other.

"My grandmom says a police inspector was at the school on registration day," Adalgiza reported.

"Ah!" Amanda exclaimed, "My mom told me that a few days ago, a burglar broke into the school. They found blood stains on the walls of that very classroom," the girl pointed at the middle room.

"Oh, yes! And that the portraits of the Heroes of Independence were all stained," Adalgiza added.

"Mama said it was a ghost. The spirit of a bandit who killed a lot of people on a farm," said Mariela, the girl with the pigtails and the gray eyes.

"But ghosts don't bleed!" Maribel noted.

"Dad says we have a new teacher," Amanda announced, making an effort to get off the topic. She appeared smaller this year.

"Any room, please! Except Doña Lola's!" Mariela pleaded.

"As long as she isn't our teacher!" Maribel proposed. She still remembered Doña Lola's punishments, her impatience, and her perennial smell of chalk. Time had changed her feelings towards the fat, dark-skinned lady, because in the end, the woman had restored her reputation as a student. But she had not overcome her anxiety at the time of learning the woman's lessons.

"Doña Lola's classroom is too dark," Nelly recalled, her eyes shining with fear despite her smile.

"How about the Abandonment Hall?" Adalgiza asked in an almost imperceptible little voice, knowing the effect she had when mentioning the sinkhole.

"Oh, no, not the A.H.!" The girls exclaimed, momentarily breaking the semicircle.

"That is a haunted room!" Mariela reminded them. All kinds of premonitions had reflected on the girls' faces when the sound of the bell froze the activities of the small student body.

And who is going to be our teacher? Maribel asked herself, looking for a friendly face among the half dozen women standing in the corridors that framed the courtyard. The white walls had been freshly painted, and the wooden floors waxed to perfection.

"Welcome to the Boyacá school," the director greeted with her best smile. And as graceful as a palm tree in her high heels, Doña Ana recited the school rules. The third-graders exchanged furtive glances mixed with a kind of timid defiance, pondering the main obstacle between them and a life full of adventures.

The school administration decided at the last minute to accommodate the students in the Abandonment Hall, while the third-grade classroom underwent some repairs. The gloomy room was situated in one of the wings of the small building, where desks, boards, and other parapets ended their useful life.

"Sit down, girls," Doña Ana instructed the twenty-odd students who made themselves comfortable in whatever seat they could find. The teacher called the list and proceeded to explain that the one who was going to be the third-grade teacher had not yet arrived.

She probably got lost on the way, Maribel thought. Maybe it was her first day as a teacher, and she felt the same as Papito did that morning.

"In the meantime, you're going to render an artistic version of some of the objects in the classroom," Doña Ana assigned them before leaving.

The assignment did not have to be repeated. Amanda displayed the beautiful, colored box that her father had bought her. The girls sat around her with the assurance that their little friend would share her colored pencils. They would draw their personal and collective version of the old board, of the desks and the atlas; of the window framing the spectacular panoramic view of the distant mountain ranges.

Maribel felt the urge to capture in her drawing the overwhelming feeling of a classroom without a teacher. Her imagination rose so high that she could at last remember and summon the spirit of the Indian boy (a goblin? a pixie?) whom she had met in the forest of her dream.

Agmmandiel! Of course!

She remembered his name, and there he was, by the window, signaling to her to release her uncontrollable need for freedom.

"Have you found the solution to the riddle?" he asked.

Maribel felt such an inner joy that she could not respond. In the midst of a nervous giggle, she wanted to confess that she had completely forgotten what the enigma was about.

Mysteriously, the old hall appeared now as a huge stage. In a spontaneous gesture, the girl reached the board and, without being able to explain why, she began to dance while Agmmandiel sang:

> *I bring gold in both my hands*
> *And to metal I give shape*
> *I'm the spirit of the tree*
> *I'm the soul of truest love*
> *I am guardian of the children*
> *I'm the one that'll always be*
> *Agmmandiel cares for the roses*
> *Agmmandiel nourishes the sage*
> *Agmmandiel serves the wild kingdom*
> *And yet, no one can see him!.*

While repeating Agmmandiel's verse, Maribel turned around pirouetting towards the door. The girl seemed to have lost track of place and time.

Attracted by this kind of ritual of freedom that her friend had undertaken, Mariela and Nelly decided to join her in the game. The collective dance had barely begun when the black and white figure of Doña Ana, with her hands on her waist, interrupted the childish inspiration.

"What's going on here? Who is responsible for this disorder?" The principal asked.

The eyes of the students fell directly on Maribel. She returned the gaze without daring to give an excuse, and in her silence, she pleaded guilty. In a secluded corner, Agmmandiel, who was playing with a piece of chalk, began to laugh in such an infectious way that, although she tried to restrain herself, Maribel could not help but join him in a chorus.

"I don't see what the joke is, insolent girl!" Doña Ana exclaimed, grabbing her by the ear and leaving the room with her.

Oh no! Please, not there! Maribel begged whoever could hear her thoughts. The principal had stopped at the door of the second-grade classroom. "Miss Sofia, I just discovered a star!" Doña Ana said, pushing the embarrassed Maribel into the room. The girl felt the eyes of the second-year students, especially those of her sister, land on her with the peskiness of mosquitoes. The laughter that followed mortified her. She wished she could bury her head in the ground, like an ostrich. For a second, her eyes met those of the new teacher.

She didn't look angry. On the contrary, her bright gray eyes betrayed an amused complicity. The youthful freckles on her face assured her that her act did not have the seriousness that Doña Ana attributed to it.

"Bring a notebook and come back so you can start working," Miss Sofia instructed, ending the illusion of independence.

"What did they do to you?" Her concerned friends asked Maribel.

"Nothing," she replied, mostly irritated. Her anger was a mixture of fear and disappointment. She didn't want to go into a classroom full of younger girls, like her sister, and meet that teacher again. Worst of all was knowing that her little sister would bring the news home.

She chose to stay in the Hall of Abandonment, afraid of the consequences. She had begun a new drawing, certain that an upset Miss Sofia would enter the classroom at any moment. She would take her back to her classroom, where she would order her to stand in a corner and write a thousand times, "I must obey my teachers." The more she thought, the longer it took the teacher to appear. The recess bell came to the girl's help.

Maribel slipped away, avoiding being seen at all costs, trying to get lost among the other girls. When she dared to look up, convinced that the danger had passed, she came across the person of Miss Sofia standing on the threshold of her classroom. Her crystal-clear gaze, like that of a spirit, confronted the girl. With a benevolent smile, the teacher restored Maribel's peace of mind.

Maribel managed to convince her little sister not to report the incident to her parents.

"So, can I have your yo-yo?" The girl took advantage.

"Sure," Maribel conceded.

VI

The Garden of the Senses

One of the secrets of life is that what is really worthwhile is what we do for others.

— **Lewis Carroll**

𝒜 new teacher arrived earlier in the week. However, the principal assigned Miss Sofia to the third-grade class. When the classroom reopened, cleaner and sunnier than ever, the girls were finally able to start their lessons.

The large window and door opened to let in the warm sunlight and the excited students. Maribel searched everywhere for the evidence surrounding the story that, for days, had been growing in her imagination. Rumors were circulating in the neighborhood that a bandit had been killed inside the school. But now the walls were spotless, whiter than the wings of the butterflies that pollinated the flowers in the garden. The floors and desks were so shiny that they invited you to caress them while watching your face reflect on them. The white walls and uniforms contrasted pleasantly with the brown of the wood, the green of the building's frames, and the bright array of colors of the flowers.

There were the framed vellums of the national heroes: Policarpa Salavarrieta, Antonia Santos, Manuela Beltrán, Francisco de Paula Santander, and Francisco José de Caldas. And yes. Maribel thought she saw a red line crossing the face of the wise Caldas. Apparently, no one else could see it. Perhaps it was just the invisible signature of the ghost.

"As third-graders, you have to share the responsibility of making school a pleasant place," Miss Sofia said, "so I'm going to ask you to bring your favorite plant to class and keep it here for the rest of the year. We are going to take care of them in a very special way," she said, asking for four volunteers to form the gardening committee. Maribel raised her hand.

Sofía Cruz Trejos had started her job as an educator well. She was accompanied by a wonderful sense of humor and an exceptional talent for teaching history and science. For the first time in her student life, Maribel had a teacher who encouraged her to think and enjoy while learning. Until now, her teachers had taken instruction so seriously that they had managed to intimidate her.

Miss Sofia wore light makeup and smelled of gentle soaps. The girls had noticed that the first thing the young lady did when she entered the classroom was to take off her heels and put on a pair of orange Indian loafers adorned with bright nuggets. They were the most beautiful shoes they had ever seen.

The teacher opened the history class by telling them about the harvest of patriots, who had contributed with their lives to the independence of their country. Among them were a number of women who had been tortured to death, their bodies scattered throughout the national territory, seeking to discourage the rebels. Even so, they had freed the homeland from the Spaniard's yoke, and their example inspired the new generations.

Maribel turned nine, sure that all her questions would soon have an answer. She had already learned in her science class about the scientific process. Yet, there was an elusive word, which she had to find and which would open a way like a magic key... to where?

***

"Ma, when am I going to take my first communion?" Maribel felt that it was time for her to talk about the important matter.

"Soon," Herminia answered most casually.

"But, Ma, all the girls in class took it already. I'm the only one who hasn't, and I'm already nine years old. Doña Ana mocks me, asking whether I am waiting for the day I get married."

"Tell that lady that unless she's willing to pay for the dress, not to meddle in what is none of her business!"

"I can take the host in my Sunday uniform. This is how Gabriela Valencia did it. Her family could not buy her a dress."

Herminia looked at her daughter, most offended. "You and your sister will take your first communion when we get the money to make you a nice dress."

"The St. Joseph's parish is preparing for confessions," the girl insisted.

"You're going to confess at the Franciscan church," her mother stated.

"Miss Sofia says that the ceremony is essential because I shall receive the body and soul of Christ for the first time. Amanda told me that she felt like she was on cloud nine when she received the host," Maribel said longingly.

"You won't notice the difference. You already live on a cloud," replied her mother.

***

Berta Castillo, the girl who sat to her right, not only came from another school but had been born in another city, perhaps in another country, and who knows, possibly in another planet. She was so radically different from all the other girls Maribel had met at school. An extraordinary case, since the students of the Boyacá school all came from the same neighborhood.

Maribel didn't know many black girls. In fact, the only one she had seen until then had been in her first grade. Perla, Doña Lola's niece, is the daughter of an education auditor. She had been born on the Pacific coast. Her stepmother and stepsister were both white, but her mother, now deceased, and her father were both black, like Doña Lola.

Unlike Doña Lola's or her niece's, Berta's dark hair was straight and silky. Her skin was also lighter than chocolate, more of a cinnamon hue; her facial features were more refined. The girl had become popular overnight, not only because of her exotic accent, which emphasized a frenulum, but also because of her sense of drama and her ability to tell the stories of her wide repertoire: folk tales, legends, and even jokes. She told them with such ease that sometimes Maribel believed that the girl had lived them all.

During embroidery class, the third-graders surrounded Berta's desk, and while working on Mother's Day tablecloths, the girls listened, entranced, to Berta weave her fanciful stories.

Miss Sofia began to suspect that the reason for the poorly kept secret of the boisterous meetings was the incessant whispering of the Castillo girl, followed by the surprised faces, the shrugged shoulders, the frightened exclamations, and the laughter of her listeners.

Maribel had stopped her work to react to Berta's most recent story when she felt the inexplicable and overwhelming force of the fabulous tales that snatch the imagination of schoolgirls during those special moments of the day.

***

One by one, Maribel and her friends descended into the clearing of the forest that Berta was describing. There was a blue sky and a sunny moment of greens as intense as the song of the cicadas. The girls watched in wonder at the lively activity around them. The watercolor vegetation and multiple designs began to look familiar. They reminded them of the childish panorama they had drawn on the adventurous day in the Abandonment Hall.

"Look!" Adalgiza pointed out in surprise, "The squirrel in a tree I painted!" The funny thing was that, now, it had a life of its own.

A henhouse and a pigsty with very plump pigs; a cow winked at them; multicolored kites with long tails, foamy clouds, so white and fat! They looked like a herd of sheep. The girls were floating, unable to keep their feet on the ground.

"The little sheep I painted for Mother's Day!" Amanda exclaimed.

"Welcome to the Garden of the Senses!" A voice seemingly originated from a flower, which added:

"Whatever you call with your thoughts, you will be able to experience with your senses."

"Everything? Even unpleasant things?" Adalgiza cowered at the possibility.

"Even a fart?" Mariela proposed, and it didn't take long for the bad smell to invade the atmosphere.

"Ugh! What a killjoy you are, Mariela!" Adalgiza complained.

"And now, how do we get rid of this stench?" asked an annoyed Amanda.

"Think of something that smells good, quick!" Nelly suggested.

"Rotten fish!" Berta joked. And the foul smell replaced the old one, making the girls jump in despair.

"No! Let it smell like an angel!" said Amanda.

"What does an angel smell like?" Adalgiza tried to figure it out.

"The most delicious thing in this world," Berta said.

"Hmm! It smells of jasmines!" Berta sniffed with delight.

"And of bubble gum!" Mariela smiled.

"It smells of colognes and baby oil, of chocolate and vanilla ice cream!" Adalgiza whispered, and everything was a festival for the sense of smell.

"It smells of Sundays!" Maribel decided.

Frankincense and myrrh smelled of churches and palaces. They heard bells tolling with a heavenly melody. In the midst of the ding-dongs, Maribel heard a well-known laugh.

"Agmmandiel!" she thought and then exclaimed: "Oh, my God, where have they all gone?" Her friends had all disappeared!

"Have you found the key to the enigma?" The answer seemed very important to the boy.

He was still the mischievous-looking indigenous boy she had met in her dreams, but now he dressed with less fanfare. His clothing was simply a loincloth and sandals. There were no feathers or flowers in his attire. The sun made his skin look the color of cinnamon and the texture of silk. A white Angora cat was by his side!

"Micifú, what are you doing here?" Maribel was surprised to see Mamita's cat.

"It's a good thing you're not with the dwarves!" said the elf with relief.

Maribel recalled the reason for Agmmandiel's antipathy for Longtooth.

"Do you say that because of what he did to you?" She said, crossing her fingers as she had seen the old gnome do.

Agmmandiel covered his ears in pain, kicked the ground, and shouted angrily:

"Let go! You silly girl!"

"I'm so sorry!" said Maribel, uncrossing her fingers. She had just realized that the elf was as vulnerable as she was.

"Don't do that again! It hurts!" He sounded quite angry.

All of a sudden, as fast as they had disappeared, her friends appeared in front of them.

"Oh, what a divine place!" Mariela exclaimed, as if she had been far away.

"This must be heaven," Amanda sighed.

Mariela noticed the boy and asked, "Who is he?"

"He looks just like my brother!" Nelly commented.

"This is my friend, Agmmandiel," Maribel informed them proudly.

"Agmman—what?" Berta was amused by the name.

Agmmandiel did not seem aware of the girls because he addressed Maribel alone: "You must solve the riddle soon if you want to meet Akum."

"I don't know if I can," the girl confessed.

"Why not?" He was disappointed.

"Because I have no idea..."

"You humans are hopeless!" he was convinced.

"Not true! I've been busy preparing for my first communion!"

"I love first communions!" Agmmandiel said excitedly.

"Well, give me a clue, and you can come to the celebration!"

"We can make a deal," he said.

"A deal?"

"I'll wait until the ceremony for you to solve the riddle!"

This could be an interesting game. She could prove to Agmmandiel that she wasn't slow or lazy. She was about to agree when the boy and cat vanished.

"Is he really your friend?" Her classmates were impressed.

"Enter the Garden of Sounds," the gentle voice of a palm tree invited.

"Who said that?" asked a frightened Mariela.

"Don't be so loud, please, Miss Sofia can hear us," Adalgiza reminded them.

A most charming chant of contagious rhythm gave way to the colors of the rainbow.

"It's the musical scale!" Berta discovered.

"What would happen if we sang?" Maribel wondered.

"Never mind! Let's sing!" Berta challenged them.

> *My donkey*
> *my donkey*
> *has hurt his ears*
> *the doctor has prescribed him*
> *a glass full of beer.*

"Look! There's the donkey, up there!" Adalgiza laughed uncontrollably as the animal flew around her, leaving a bright trail of gilded colors.

"Wait until Miss Sofia hears us sing," said Nelly, "let's sing *The Nightingale!*"

"No, that song is sorrowful," Adalgiza said a little too late, because a bird appeared, trapped in the thorns of a rose bush.

"Someone is out of tune! I don't know of any purple nightingales!" Amanda observed.

They sang *La Campesina,* a beautiful girl dressed in a muslin costume, singing happily like an oriole.

"I'd love to eat popcorn," Amanda wished.

"Then you must go to the Garden of Flavors," they heard a plant say.

"This place is enchanted," Mariela acknowledged.

The girls were not intimidated and entered a field where popcorn fell like manna from heaven. They ran everywhere trying to catch the crisps in the fabric of their uniforms. Mariela changed the widespread desire for the taste of her favorite ice cream. Flowers and plants were soon transformed into a gallery of sugar cones containing all flavors and colors of ice cream. Nelly picked up vanilla cream cookies while Adalgiza quenched her thirst in a fountain of mandarin juice.

"I wish we could stay here forever," Mariela wished.

"No, we don't want to do that," said Berta cautiously, "we'd get fat and boring."

"Where is your friend?" Nelly wandered.

"Is he your Guardian Angel?" Amanda ventured.

"He looks more like an elf," Mariela said.

"He must be a genie," Adalgiza dared.

"And what is all this about an enigma? Tell us," Berta prompted Maribel.

The same force that had swept her away from the classroom deposited her back on her chair without anyone noticing. Maribel found herself trying to follow the pattern of the tablecloth with her needle and her red Calabrian thread, while listening to Berta conclude the story of the giant Seven Leagues.

Maribel looked around and saw her friends laboriously working.

VII

The Path of Flowers

There are those who consider themselves perfect,
but it is only because they demand less of themselves.

— Hermann Hesse

"*W*hen I was a boy," said her father, taking advantage of the fact that everyone was at the table, "there were no comforts, much less compassion for the students. We studied with old books, that is, if we were lucky enough to find them or inherit them from an older brother. But if you were as poor as I was, who didn't even have siblings, you had to study without books of any kind."

Rigoberto Morales was convinced that no one—with the exception of Marco Fidel Suárez, the humble boy who became president of the Republic—had gone through as much work as he did when he was young. During his childhood, he had managed to go to school barefoot, as he had no shoes. He had rarely written on paper, because it was so expensive that it could only be paid for with gold. To waste it, apart from being senseless, was worthy of punishment.

The law that prevailed at that time was: A student learned best if he was spanked frequently. The teacher—he remembered—had a license to treat a student like a circus beast. Today's students were more fortunate because educators had learned to use the punishment rule without leaving bloody marks.

"The students of my generation did really love to learn," he concluded his brief speech, and applied to eating his beef and vegetable soup before it cooled.

Maribel couldn't forget that afternoon's history class. Miss Sofia had told them about the education that El Libertador and Father of the Nation had received. His tutor—she told them—taught him without the strict discipline of colonial times.

Don Simón Rodríguez taught the orphan boy— who would one day liberate five nations—in the countryside, among trees and flowers, rivers, and mountains. Bolívar discovered the wonders of this world, learned to respect nature, and to love freedom. The desire to travel awakened in him early in life. Under the tutelage of his teacher, he would learn that knowledge nourishes man's ideals and freedom nourishes the spirit and imagination, but that there can only be progress where there is education. One day, on the top of a mountain, that boy, now a man, would swear before his mentor not to give rest to his arm or to his soul, until he saw his country free from the oppressive yoke.

"Persistence is the key to success," declared Rigoberto.

"I don't like school at all!" Papito announced, causing a family stir.

"The worse for you! You'll waste the fortune of being in a private school," his father replied.

"When I grow up, I'm going to join a circus," said the child, provoking the laughter of his family.

"I hope you learn fast how to brush a lion's teeth," said his father.

***

It was a little after one o'clock when the girls began to gather at the school entrance. It was a good excuse to chat with your friends. Friendship depended on how close you lived to each other or where you sat in class. Amanda had brought some of the comics her brother collected and shared with Maribel, while treating her to the breadsticks that the old man sold at the tiny candy stand.

"It's a miracle you made it so early, Adalgiza!" Amanda commented without taking her eyes off her reading.

"Don't say that!" Maribel poked her friend with an elbow. Adalgiza's usually neatly combed reddish hair appeared all tangled and in a complete disarray.

"My grandmother pulled my hair when she was combing it." She was on the verge of tears.

"Does your grandmother still comb your hair?" Maribel was surprised.

"She helps me, that's it! But today she was annoyed because I told her that I was leaving early. She's worried because my youngest uncle was drafted. She says a lot of soldiers have been killed lately."

"My mom believes my grandma spoils us too much," Amanda said.

"Don't pay attention to this girl," Maribel advised Adalgiza, and her attention was diverted by Nelly's arrival, escorted by her older brother.

"Nelly's brother is so cute," Amanda sighed.

"He's too aloof!" Adalgiza said, trying to ignore him.

Mariela arrived soon after Nelly's brother left. Her intention was to sit alone, but the girls gathered around her, all worried.

"What's wrong?" Amanda asked.

The question prompted Mariela's inconsolable tears.

"Did your mother hit you again?" Maribel assumed, pointing to the marks on the child's skinny legs.

"Poor thing," Adalgiza exclaimed, passing her hand through the girl's ashen dark hair.

"That's why my mom left my dad," Berta said, approaching the group.

Nelly frowned while listening to her classmates. She had never been beaten by her parents. But then again, they had died when she was very young. Still, nobody would dare to do that in her family.

Adalgiza complained about her grandmother's slaps: "They annoy me more than they hurt!"

"My dad never punishes us, and Mom, only when there is a reason," Amanda confided.

"Mom whips me with a cord," Mariela admitted between sobs.

"My God! Look at those welts. You have to put some ointment on them," Maribel suggested.

"Heal, heal, little ass, if it doesn't heal today, it will heal tomorrow!" Berta recited, making Mariela smile and forget her sadness for a moment.

The girls watched Miss Sofia apply cocoa butter to Mariela's wounds, while Doña Ana commented:

"It's time to talk to that lady about the way she punishes her daughter."

***

The schoolyard was framed on two sides by the corridors and classrooms, on the other side by the white wall adjacent to a house, and on the fourth side by the teachers' toilets, the students' septic tank, and a water tank. It had been there in front of that washing tank, where Edilma Duque had taught Maribel to whistle. It had cost her a bottle of blue ink, but it had been a good investment. She was very proud of the melodious sounds she could make nowadays.

There were flowers of all colors in the garden, which was occasionally visited by a couple of hummingbirds, a few adventurous bees, and numerous butterflies. Maribel had just learned in science class about the incredible metamorphosis that turned the humble caterpillar into an elegant butterfly.

There, in the patio, Amanda and Adalgiza competed to see who could volley the highest. *Volear* was an amateur trapeze act in which the volleyer started swirling, holding a girl by her hands, until her teammate was floating.

It was Maribel's turn to fly, and Adalgiza grabbed her hands as hard as she could. Slowly, she initiated the circling with her human cargo, reaching maximum speed in a short time. Maribel took off from the ground, firmly attached to her friend. For a brief moment, *she felt weightless and started to float.* A second later, she felt the world had crashed on her.

Her body had impacted the ground. She was breathless and in a state of shock. Her skin and impeccable white uniform were smeared with dirt. But all she could concentrate on was the dark reddish stains and scrapes on her knees and hands and the feeling of burning. The most intense pain came after the blow. Her left arm, which she had instinctively used to cushion the fall, had dislocated.

Alarmed, Doña Ana and Miss Sofia came out of their classrooms when they heard the screams.

"What a lousy landing!" was Doña Ana's comment when she saw that her student was alive.

"You'd better go home," Miss Sofia advised.

Maribel felt deserted. She knew she would be in serious trouble with her mom if she got home in that condition.

Amanda was more concerned and acted more responsibly. "Let's go to my house. My dad will help you."

"No! I'm fine! I just need to clean up!" Maribel exclaimed, faced with the scary thought of meeting Don Arturo.

Rumors in the neighborhood were that he was a shaman, a *curandero,* and thus he practiced witchcraft.

But her arm was beginning to hurt so much that she finally let herself be led by her friend.

They left school, Maribel shielded by Amanda to avoid being seen, holding her left arm with her right and making an effort not to let the tears flow.

In a couple of minutes that seemed like hours, they arrived at Amanda's home.

The door was open and led to a dark hall and a row of stairs. Maribel felt faint when they walked to the ground floor. She noticed the silhouettes of a chair and a desk in the background. The wood creaked at their every step.

Amanda told her to stay put and was about to go upstairs to brief her parents when the woman's voice came from upstairs.

"What happened, *mi niña*? Why did you return from school?"

"Don't worry. It's Mom," Amanda reassured her.

"Did you forget something?" The lady asked when they reached the second floor.

"Mom, please tell Daddy that Maribel injured her arm."

There was the scent of wax all over the house. The hardwood floors were as clean and polished as tanned mirrors. The furniture was simple but cozy and of pleasant colors. There was a large plant in a corner and a classical portrait of the Sacred Heart of Jesus on one of the walls of the room.

A middle-aged man with oriental features stood by the door of a studio. He wore thick glass lenses and looked through them, trying to guess what had happened.

"It was an accident, *papi!* She crashed while volleying," Amanda explained.

Don Arturo looked at her with compassion. Maribel sighed as *she modified in her mind the figure of a hunchback with warts and a large nose she had imagined.* He was thin, even skinny, and much older than her father. He looked a lot like she imagined Chan Li Po, the Chinese detective of the *radionovela.*

The healer remained silent when he examined Maribel's arm, settling it on his hand, delicately, as if holding a flower.

"Take off her uniform," said Doña Leonor to her daughter. "I'll wash and clean her skin."

Amanda took charge, and when Maribel was free of the uniform and the dirt, Don Arturo led her to his office.

Taking the girl gently by the waist, he sat her on the table near the window. Then he opened a drawer and took out a small bottle of balm, cotton, and a tube of ointment. She was able to immediately identify the smell of her mom's favorite remedy for home accidents. He rubbed the oil on her hands and knees with the cotton and put band-aids on the most visible wounds.

"You won't be able to hide the truth from your mom, you know," he said, looking intently into her eyes.

She knew it, but she didn't care anymore. Don Arturo examined her arm once more, red, swollen, scratched. *She was confused by her own curiosity to know if this gentleman was really a witch or a sorcerer.*

The healer's face was definitely that of a Chinese person. With his bushy, disheveled eyebrows, his little eyes framed by glasses that looked to her like a toy. The aquiline nose was an exact copy of

Amanda's and perhaps of the rest of his family. The thin lips were even thinner because his teeth refused to stay inside his mouth. His chin was small, almost weak. His Adam's apple stood out so much that it was comical to see it rise and fall every time he swallowed.

Maribel sought to escape her pain. Her attention clung with great effort to everything in sight: the plants that hung from the ceiling and appeared to her as wigs of assorted greens. The bottles and jugs, capsules, and boxes, arranged like small books in a fairy library, gave the room the appearance of a fascinating pharmacy.

She had seen all kinds of plants at the market's botany section, where her grandma bought the medicinal herbs that the Pijaos natives sold.

"Does it hurt?" He stared at her as if helping her face the pain. Maribel nodded, and her eyes flooded with tears. *There was something warm about the gesture of an elderly person taking care of her.*

The healer extended the girl's fingers again with infinite care, using his hand as a base. He grabbed hers, and before she knew it, he gave it such a sudden tug that Maribel felt a current go down her back, run through her arm, past her wrist, and reach the tip of her fingers.

"Does it hurt now?" Amanda's father asked her with interest.

Maribel nodded. She felt her arm fall asleep, but the pain had disappeared by the work and grace of this man she mistook for a sorcerer.

"What would you have done if you had been able to fly?" He asked her with a smile.

Maribel didn't know. Perhaps she would have gone to an unknown place and stayed there to explore. She would have loved to visit the tribes that had inhabited the regions of Quindío centuries ago, those people with a history so rich in legends that *she would have been fascinated to listen.*

She remembered that it was time to go back to school. Doña Leonor had washed her uniform, and Amanda had brought one, no longer worn by her sister, for Maribel to wear.

"Do you like plants?" Don Arturo asked her. "Yes," she answered, surprised to be able to make a sound. "My grandma has many at home."

"Plants help heal those who care for them," he said.

"That's what Mamita says," she smiled at him.

The healer opened a jar with a refreshing scent of menthol. He applied the ointment on her arm and rubbed it with energy.

"They say that angels designed the plant kingdom. During the creation of the world, they painted, individually, their own plant and flower."

Of course! That was what Agmmandiel did, she realized. "Wasn't that what the enigma said? That he lived among flowers and took care of them!"

"Ready, miss! Your wing is in a position to fly again," Don Arturo joked. "Tell your mom to apply this ointment on your arm for seven days."

"Why seven?" She was intrigued.

"Because seven is a magic number!"

***

Almost a week had passed since the accident. Although her mom had scolded her for not being careful, she had been kind to her all those days. She soon realized the reason: her mother was expecting a baby, and to celebrate it, she and her sister would take their first communion on the day of the *Virgen del Carmen*.

Maribel was overjoyed. She was happy to think that there would be another baby in the house, even though the fact was no longer the news. For her, it was that she would finally take the host at her First Communion.

Herminia was so moved that she summoned the memory of her own. She was Maribel's age when she had gone to church and received communion before her day. When she went to church on that special date wearing her white dress, it was the second time she had taken the host. Still, she considered it her rehearsal. Her daughters would have to be a model of kindness from that moment on.

The mountains were foggier than ever, and the river swelled with the rains. The bridge, however, seemed small in the middle of the lush nature. The house by the river, from afar, looked like a toy. In fact, her own house—the dining room, the chairs, her hiding place—seemed to be shrinking. She no longer fit in the places accessible to Micifú.

Maribel and Miriam recited the prayers their mother and grandmother had taught them. They were prayers to remind them of their mortality and to teach them humility before God, no matter how much suffering was destined for them.

Maribel preferred to pray to her guardian angel. Such prayers spoke of faith and goodness, and above all, of mercy. Angels were in charge of the miracles necessary to rescue humans from evil.

"Oh, my guardian angel, my sweet companion," Maribel repeated that night, mixing her wishes with her prayers. In her dreams, she looked at the river again. She saw the little people of the flowers, then a shadow, followed by a light, and finally the youthful figure of an incredibly attractive being, supremely picaresque, definitely fantastic.

He had the most beautiful of faces, the most refined of bodies, draped with flowers and leaves. She saw the spirit—there was no other way to call it—playing with the colors of dreams, wanting to teach her about the undulating waters of the El Quindío River.

Agmmandiel inspired her to learn about the life of the trees, the names of the elementals, and the guardians of each and every one of the manifestations in the universe. Above all, he communicated to her the secret that grown-ups keep forever in their memories: that the earth is the planet of childhood.

***

It was sunny and cool in the morning when, armed with a hoe, a spear, and a shovel, Mamita went down to her patio with a bagful of kernels of maize and began turning the earth to sow it. She had learned since her youth in the countryside about the symmetry of planting: Leave enough room so that when the plants and then the ears grow, they wouldn't get so crowded that they'd suffocate.

Maribel offered to help her grandma, who, in spite of the fact that the girl sometimes fell asleep on top of the corn grinder while cooking arepas, she still had enough confidence in her.

"What are the beans for, Granny?" she asked, watching Grandma mix the grains.

"They help the corn plant grow bigger and stronger."

Would it be possible? But she wasn't going to discuss the crazy possibility that ears of beans would come off the plant and not the corn, as Grandma expected.

"And how long do we have to wait?" she asked instead.

"About seven weeks," answered *la abuela*.

"Mamita, is it true that the Indians buried *guacas* in this land?"

"True!" She replied without hesitation.

"And do we have one buried in this courtyard?"

"Who knows, *mi hijita*. But if there were one, the blessed souls would let us know."

"Are we poor, Grandma?"

"No, *mi hija*! We are rich in spirit."

"But to be poor means not to be able to have what you want, isn't it?"

"And don't you think that happens to the rich, too?"

"Do you know what I would do if I found a *guaca*?" It wasn't really a question, but her invitation to fantasy. "I would buy a house for Mom, a business for Dad, a farm for you, and I'd give money to Tía Marina."

"How many guacas do you expect to find, *mi hija?*"

"Well, seven, of course. And I'll spend my fortune to travel around the world."

Maribel had begun to put away the spear when she noticed that her brother, who until that moment had been playing around, was trampling on the crops and adopting an alarming position.

"Mamita! Papito is peeing on the flowers!" She warned her grandmother, who was already on her way to stop the boy.

Caught in the middle of the act, Papito started to run.

Holding the spear, Maribel followed Mamita, trying to keep her balance as the terrain grew rougher. The natural tilt of the Earth caused her to lose her balance. The girl slipped beyond the boundaries of the courtyard, where the earth lost its firmness and became a rolling place. She tried to hold on to the spear, but the girl continued to roll quickly towards the river.

"Hold on to a branch, *mi hijita!*" Mamita shouted, terrified.

Maribel let go of the spear so that she could even touch the unreachable branches. In her desperation, she invoked Agmmandiel.

She saw the boy standing with open arms and legs, as if waiting to stop her fall. Suddenly, a giant wild plant intercepted her body. Slowly, leaning against the spear, Maribel ascended to the patio, where her grandmother was thanking all the saints in heaven.

Once on the balcony of her house, Mamita rewarded her granddaughter with a frothy cup of chocolate and a large *arepa*.

"Well, now we must wait for the maize to sprout!" she exclaimed.

"And for the baby to be born," Maribel sighed.

She longed for her first communion, as she looked at the beautiful furrows that she and her *abuela* had sown.

Now she needed to talk seriously to Agmmandiel.

VIII

The Valley of Ghosts

What is an adult? A child inflated by age.
— **Simone de Beauvoir**

"*W*ould you give us one of your children?" asked the handsome young man standing at the door of the Morales home. He was accompanied by a very pretty woman. The friendly visitors made Herminia smile.

Josué and Deyanira's visit was as unforeseen as it was full of joy for the children. The couple, who couldn't have the child they longed for, frequented their home, perhaps to get a feeling of a big family. The children called them aunt and uncle, and no one questioned the relationship because, family or not, their visits caused a stir.

Josué was a construction worker who had the talents of a radio announcer and the figure of a movie star. He could have been a poet or a singer, but Herminia said that he would have been considered an irresponsible husband, and he and his wife would have surely starved.

Deyanira resembled one of those Mexican actresses Maribel had seen in the movies and the collection of glossy photos Tía Marina kept in her trunk. Always by Josué's side, she was a team player, supporting his stories, providing him with background sounds and comments. They had married very young but acted like newlyweds. They enjoyed the world of children and seemed to have fun together.

"Choose the one you want," Herminia told them, inviting them in.

"Let's go see, Deyanira," he said, studying the small faces, "who do we want best?"

"Give us a little girl," she said.

"Someday you'll know what it's really like to raise children," the mother wished and warned them. "Then you'll be back and ask me to keep yours."

Sitting in the living room, surrounding the couple, wondering if it was true that they wanted to take one of them away, Maribel, Miriam, Papito, and little Lucy did not dare to move from their posts. They feared their mother's decision, or worse, the announcement that they had to go to bed and thus miss the horror stories that Josué was about to tell.

"When I was a chick," he began, "I worked on the farm with my old man, after spending a few hours in school. It's not that my dad believed that studying was less productive, but he always thought that one learned faster by working. From a very young age, he taught me how to sow. He said that one learns patience by waiting for the harvest. On the side, while picking the coffee beans or the corn ears, one learned to tell the dew from the witches' spit and to locate their dwellings."

"Yes, the witches spat on the leaves, and you had to be very careful not to touch their poisonous saliva. At night, the cursed ones stood on the roofs of the houses, the very harpies, like nocturnal birds accompanied by the tenebrous sounds of the owls and grasshoppers."

"I'm sleepy," Papito announced.

While the mother carried the child to bed, Miriam came to sit next to Maribel to hold on to her every time Josué and Deyanira changed the tone of their voices or mentioned the names of the terrible creatures that inhabited the forest.

Maribel felt her blood freeze when Josué described the valley, the same one that could be seen from the balcony, their lookout to the river. By day, it was bright, but by night, a sea of dark shadows, as the narrator described: no moon, no stars, no hope. By day and seen from afar, the river was an incredible sight, a beautiful and vigorous silver road. At night and hidden in the thicket, it was the roaring menace of a giant black panther.

A cold wind whipped the trees and whistled in their ears, while wet hands seemed to caress the frightened bodies—macabre whispers that sounded ghostly in the hoots of owls and other nocturnal birds. Josué's voice was cavernous, as the only company in that stormy valley whose endless bottom was the river.

Holding hands, the two girls hurried away before midnight arrived, the moment when terror would be the master of the night, and they would fall into its clutches without hope of salvation.

Suddenly, when they were already sensing the faint light of the shack by the river and breathing a little more confidently, a creature appeared in front of them.

"A chick!" Miriam exclaimed, delighted.

The little creature looked stray. They followed it; at times it appeared closer, yet, suddenly, it was far away. In time, Maribel remembered what Amanda had revealed to her.

"It's the evil chick!" She whispered to her sister. *It was the nocturnal creature that led people astray to trap them in the depths of the valley. They would appear dead or drowned in the river the next day.*

"No, let's not follow it! Pray! If we see it closely, it'll already be gone."

"Isn't it the other way around?"

"No! It is a deception!"

They both made the sign of the cross and invoked aloud the name of Jesus. When they seemed to have escaped the evil chick, a persistent stomp frightened them. *La Patasola!*

Maribel ran, her heart pounding in her chest. She fell, got up, cried, prayed, suddenly realizing that her sister had disappeared. She felt a lump in her throat, so tight that she couldn't swallow. *What was their mother going to say to her? She, the eldest, responsible for her younger siblings, had been a coward. She had abandoned her sister.*

"Agmmandiel! For God's sake! Help my little sister get home safely!"

The horrible and persistent stomp of la Patasola chased her to the river. She could hear Josué's voice like an echo in the distance.

After a while, she heard the water and the current breaking on the rocks. She was almost relieved when a grotesque and deformed woman emerged from the currents. It had a diabolical face with pointed ears. Although she was crying, she seemed to mock the girl.

"My child! My child!" The woman moaned, raising her bloody hands. The girl recognized the *Madremonte.* Her laugh was so cruel that it made her hair stand on end. Maribel yelled for her sister.

She could only hear Josué's voice.

"Beware!" he was saying, "you could be the next victim!"

Josué was now in the middle of the living room, saying, "We all are afraid of the dark. The key is to have the courage to handle fear and not let fear drive us."

"Where is Miriam?!" Maribel asked worriedly, afraid to tell her mother that she had lost her in The Valley of Ghosts and wishing with all her soul that she had found the way.

"She fell asleep, and I took her to bed," her mother explained. Maribel breathed a sigh of relief. *"Thank you, Agmmandiel!"* and deep down *she vowed never to doubt her friend ever again.*

"Please don't let me dream of those monsters," she begged the Virgin Mary that night.

The tales of Josué and Deyanira were worth a treasure of long-lasting memories. They were important lessons for surviving in this life. Stories that illustrated good and evil, those two forces which humans must perennially confront, as different from each other as day and night, and yet part of the same world. They were wise stories contained in the universal mind, which the younger ones were just beginning to recognize.

Maribel envied her siblings for having been able to fall asleep. She remained very still in her bed, her gaze fixed on the lamp that illuminated the holy image. Her eyes veiled with fatigue, she tried to ignore the restless shadows that moved before her, thinking about whether courage would be the magic word to solve Agmmandiel's enigma.

IX

The Bridge of Illusions

*It is a wonderful fact and worthy of reflection on it,
that each of the human beings is a profound secret to others.*

— **Charles Dickens**

Many sounds mingled in her dream. It was night, but the valley was no longer dark or cold. Moonlight allowed her to walk without fear. Maribel felt the presence of Agmmandiel by her side. She walked for a while before reaching the bridge. It was the same bridge she saw every day from the balcony of her house. Tonight, it looked newly built, and as if someone had taken the trouble to paint it and adorn it with vines and flowers.

"May I cross over?" Maribel asked the elf when he peeked out from among the flowers.

"Sure! Don't be afraid. Bridges are made to be crossed," he told her.

Yet *she was still afraid of falling, of not being able to get to the other side.*

"Do these flowers fall?" Agmmandiel pointed to her. The vegetation seemed to come alive and multiply to form a beautiful network on the bridge path.

"If they sense your fear, they will refuse to let you pass," the boy explained.

"What can I do?" Maribel didn't want to go back.

"A single word will open the way again," her guide invited. On the other side was the mountain of Akum.

The girl didn't know what to say. She was there, in front of the wonderful bridge that would lead her to the magical place. *If only she knew the password!* "I think I have a clue," she said, unsurely. *Was it a word or a number?* She listed in her mind the possible ones she had gathered: persistence? Courage? Seven? Nothing moved.

Maribel looked around for the sign that would let her know if the clues had a chance, but Agmmandiel had vanished. *She was sobbing when she began the way back.*

Suddenly, on the road, stationed at a walking distance, she saw a man who was taking care of half a dozen geese. He greeted her, raising his hand, as if he knew her. *She realized she knew him, too.*

"Hello," he said, approaching her. The man was Chinese and wore a white silk gown embroidered with the figure of a dragon in red. On his head, a cap that allowed her to see his long, black hair, braided in a thin tail and tied with a ribbon, resembling the tail of a kite.

"Hello! Missie," he said with a strong accent and the friendliest of attitudes. "Did you solve the riddle?"

"How do you know...?"

"I know you haven't succeeded.... *Hmmm, pa-*tience! Lots of patience!"

"You are Chan Li Po!"

"Not important! What matters now is key to the enigma."

"Do you know Akum?"

"Certainly," replied the detective, adding, "I am a dutiful assistant."

"Thank you, Mr. Chan."

"You say you have clues?"

"Well, yes... I suppose. Agmmandiel says it's a single word. And I've been hunting for important words when adults talk or when I read. My dad says persistence is the key to success. Josué thinks it's courage. Don Arturo says that seven is a magic number."

"Very clever! Number seven, favorite of nature. But none of those are passwords. Another clue?"

"Well, Agmmandiel's riddle says that he carries gold in his hands and he can shape metals," the girl recalled.

"Yes, yes," Chan smiled with satisfaction, "like *Muiscas!*"

"What does he mean by: 'I am the spirit of the tree; I am the spirit of love'?"

"He inspires everything and everyone."

"I'm the angel of the children, I'm the same I've always been?"

"Life without children, very sad, indeed."

"He lives in the rose and takes care of flowers, yet no one can see him?"

"Yes, you have to imagine, to be able to see..."

Raising his hand, Chan Li Po wrote in the air with his right index, the magic word. As he was writing, he spoke: "Confucius said: *He who has knowledge without imagination is like a bird with no wings.*"

Imagination? Was that the key? Of course! With the help of Chan Li Po, she was able to deduce that *imagination* was the word with the most possibilities.

"Thank you very much, Mr. Chan. I am so very grateful!"

Maribel ran up the hill. It was getting late, and she had to get up early because tomorrow was a very important day in her life. She would go to church to confess for the first time, the prelude to the wonderful day when she would receive her first communion. And it was the day when, if imagination was the key, she could meet Akum.

Thanks to the Chinese detective, she already had the magic word that would allow her to cross the Bridge of Illusions, the word that would, perhaps, open all the doors behind which an extraordinary world full of surprises awaited her.

***

It was still dawn when the girls headed to church. They were accompanied by Julieta, the neighbor's daughter, who had already taken her first communion and therefore was experienced in the matter.

The weather was cold, and the boulevard was empty. The three girls spoke in whispers as they walked so as not to wake anyone up.

"Mom wants us to take our first communion in *Nuestra Señora del Carmen* because she believes friars are humbler than priests," Maribel informed her friend.

"Also, the church is prettier," Miriam added.

"I took my first communion there," Julieta agreed.

"The teachers at school believe we should take it in the parish," Maribel said.

"But Mom doesn't want us to," Miriam said, rejoicing at the decision.

"I didn't want to take it there either," Maribel said, remembering the terrible event that had happened on the way to the parish: The day the body of a little girl was found behind the bushes. Rumors had it that a "monster" had abducted her.

Yes, the neighborhood of *Nuestra Señora del Carmen* was definitely safer. The church was as large as the cathedral, and it had beautiful statues and gorgeous stained-glass windows with scenes from the lives of Jesus and the apostles. Everything was spotless and tidy.

The three girls could even hear the murmur and the sound of beads passing through the fingers of the women who prayed the rosary; minutes later, a choir of boys and girls arrived to rehearse the hymns for the mass. A young couple stopped from time to time in front of the carved figures of the Stations of the Cross to reflect on the *Passion of Christ*.

The place produced such a sense of peace that some people fell asleep, lulled by the chants and the scent of myrrh. Maribel imagined angels walking through the aisles of the church.

Julieta's confidence was not enough to counteract the nervousness of the two sisters as they got in line for confession.

"There is no need to be afraid! Confession doesn't hurt," she told them. "The priests forget what you tell them as soon as they give penance and blessings."

"Really?" Maribel wasn't so sure. *Would they so easily forgive and forget her quarrels with her siblings? Would they really forgive her for missing Mass on Sunday? Or her laziness, especially when she pretended not to feel well so that she could stay in bed a while longer? Would God forgive her curiosity, which could turn her into a creature of little faith, as Father Méndez usually called people like her?*

Julieta tried to cheer up her friends by entering the dark wooden booth first. A few minutes later, she came out with a sparkling smile and an aura of sainthood.

Maribel felt butterflies in her stomach. She could hardly speak when Miriam pushed her in, under the excuse that she was the older sister. It was all dark inside except for a small light that pierced the black curtain covering the confessional. It smelled of wax, incense, and religion. As soon as she knelt down, she heard a knock on the wood. A small sliding window opened on the other side, and all she saw between her and the silhouette of a young priest was a thin wire mesh.

"I accuse myself, Father, of having sinned," she heard herself repeating the introductory phrase her mother had taught her. Breathless, she recited the short list of sins.

"Speak louder, my child," said the priest, his warm, minty breath caressing her face.

She raised her voice as loud as she could, trying to breathe normally.

When she heard the penance and saw the father make the sign of the cross, *she knew that she had been forgiven.* She took a deeper breath and left the confessional with a feeling of levitation. She looked at her little sister to assure her that the act of confession was a good thing and that penance was not really a punishment.

"I need to pee," said Miriam as she came out of the confessional.

"There are no toilets around here," Maribel reminded her, hoping that she would hold on a little.

"We can go to the cemetery," Juliet suggested.

"It's still very early!" Maribel complained.

"But I can't hold it!" Miriam exclaimed, beginning a funny ritual dance.

"Well, come on, but if a skeleton shows up, I'll be the first to run!"

The cemetery was closed, but Julieta discovered an open gap between two bars of the grille, through which they could enter.

"Hurry up!" Maribel said as soon as she crossed, and Miriam could at last relieve herself behind the slab of a large tomb.

"What are you going to hurry for?" Juliet questioned. "Mom says that the dead can do you no harm, and the living are more dangerous."

Maribel figured that Julieta's mom knew what she was talking about because she was a nurse. But what if there were live people in the cemetery?

"Well, in that case, you have to run like a soul persecuted by the devil," her friend laughed.

Such calm was suspicious. Only the sun was keeping them company. Maribel could feel the warmth of the sun's rays, giving them the courage to walk further into the cemetery.

"We may ask the souls for favors!" it occurred to Miriam.

"Better start praying, they rest in peace," Julieta recommended.

No sooner had they begun a Holy Mary than they heard a pounding in the plaza that contained the vaults.

"I told you so!" Maribel exclaimed.

"It must be the gravedigger," Juliet said, looking at the man on top of a ladder hammering at a vault.

"Why is he doing that?" Miriam asked.

"And at this time of the day!" Maribel added.

They walked cautiously toward him. The man, covering half of his face with a handkerchief that made him look like a bandit, had started to remove the pieces of concrete. He followed by clearing the dust and pulling a casket.

Very soon, they realized the reason for the handkerchief.

"Foo! It smells awful!" Miriam exclaimed, covering her nose with both hands, a gesture that Julieta and Maribel imitated.

"It's the smell of death, *muchachitas!*" said the gravedigger, his voice choked by the rag. "What are you doing here so early, girls?"

"I had to..." Miriam couldn't finish as Maribel poked her.

"We have come to pray to the blessed souls," said Julieta, particularly careful to follow her mother's instructions not to trust strangers.

"Why did you open that tomb?" Miriam asked him.

"This body has been here for seven years. Now they will cremate it and bring the ashes to the parochial crypts."

"Did you hear?" Miriam groaned, "There are dead people in the parish."

"Only their ashes," explained Julieta.

The girls watched in awe as the gravedigger lowered the coffin with the help of a rope. The mortuary box was in such poor condition that it almost fell apart before it reached the floor. They detailed the dead body, trying to hold their breath.

The gravedigger said it was the body of a young man, although it had long hair and nails. He explained that hair and nails keep growing even when one is dead.

"And how is this one going to do when resurrection comes?" Maribel inquired.

"It seems to me that it would take a miracle!" predicted the gravedigger.

"Do they pay you to dig up the dead?" asked Miriam.

"And to bury them. That's my job. I have a family to support."

***

That morning over breakfast and before leaving for school, Miriam related their journey to confession to her mom. And so, she did it in great detail.

"Don't talk about the dead while you're eating," Herminia reminded her, scolding Maribel for taking her little sister to the cemetery.

"But Ma! She had to pee! Besides, there was nothing but the dead in there!"

X

Akum's Mountain

Those who don't believe in magic will never find it.
— **Roald Dahl**

Herminia had designed and sewn the most beautiful dresses her daughters could have worn on the day of their First Communion. The girls looked like little princesses attired in their embroidered and fluffy outfits. She was very proud of her girls and of her skills as a dressmaker.

"I love the tiara," Maribel said, admiringly, as she looked at herself in the mirror.

"Wait until you see the missals!" said the mother, handing two little white-lacquered books with gilded designs.

After the tryout, Maribel went to the balcony. It was raining, and the whole valley was covered in fog. The sound of rain made *her wish to see Agmmandiel.*

"The day is near," she heard his whisper.

"I think I've found the keyword," the girl announced.

"Hmm, then, why are you so sad?"

"Because I don't know what I am going to say when I meet Akum."

"Tell him how you feel..."

"Won't he be annoyed?"

"Why would he be annoyed?"

"Older people don't have much patience with children."

"Akum loves children!"

"How should we talk to him? Is he an angel? Or, is he a saint?"

"He's the spirit of a mighty warrior. Use your intuition and your heart. Invoke the magical language of flowers."

"And how do flowers speak?"

"Say the magic words: *Selam, Selam!* And then you will know."

"And when do I say the keyword?"

"Before you cross the Bridge of Illusions."

"When will that be?"

"Your heart will tell you."

At that precise moment, Maribel was swept away by a prodigious force. This time, Agmmandiel was holding her by the hand. In a few moments, they circled the valley. She could see everything from above. She felt the mist caressing her body. The rain had stopped, and before she had time to blink, they found themselves in front of the bridge. "Oh, Agmmandiel, we didn't even get wet!"

The indigenous elf was singing his rapturous song. It was then that Maribel understood the enigma of Agmmandiel's song and the purpose of her mystic adventure.

I am the spirit of the tree/I am the spirit of love....

The girl hesitated for a moment before deciding to pronounce the word that Chan Li Po had revealed to her in her dreams. Her friend's mischievous and confident smile restored her peace of mind. She summoned all her concentration so as not to make a mistake and stood straight as in a ceremony; she raised her arms as if she were about to conduct an orchestra of cherubs, making an effort so that her voice would be heard by all creatures. Maribel shouted with all her might:

"Imagination!"

For a moment, nothing happened. But hope showed in Maribel's face, as Agmmandiel began his metamorphosis from an elf boy to celestial bird, to spirit of the imagination. It was enough of a sign that the keyword was correct.

"I did it, I did it!" She was jubilant.

Like a curtain pulled by invisible hands, the plants and flowers that had previously obstructed the way, blinding it, gracefully opened to form a grotto of marvelous colors, the ground covered with the greenest pastures. Maribel could see the rising rainbow on the other side of the mountain, Akum's realm.

"You shall go alone," her young guide announced. "And remember: this place is sacred."

Maribel crossed the bridge, slowly, stopping only to pick the most beautiful of flowers. When she reached the other side, she looked back to see Agmmandiel and regain her confidence, but the elf had disappeared.

Cautiously, she observed the landscape. Mysteriously, the mountain had split in two, and the groove, a grotto populated with phosphorescent green ferns, let in the subtle light from an unknown source. No shadows covered her path, no obstacle; she perceived the silent harmony that sometimes seemed musical to her. She was beginning to get used to the stillness of the mountain, the iridescent texture of the rocks, and the unearthly softness of the ground on which she was walking, when the current of a spring alerted her.

A looming phenomenon stirred the birds in their nests and other animals in their dens and caves. The majestic presence appeared gradually before her eyes. The imposing height, the fantastic tunic contrasting with the plumage adorning his headset, were worthy of the legend. *Was he a prophet? A magician? A warrior? All of that?*

Maribel could appreciate the bravery of the *Muisca* race in the face framed by the colorful feathers and the golden structure dotted with brightly colored gems. The lucidity of that outfit allowed the seer to estimate the hands of the spinners who had woven the tunic and sandals. The girl could feel the spiritual essence of the *Cacique* that emerged from the plate of a historical tome. Hearing the footstep of his sandal evoked scenes of the faith that had built an empire.

"I was waiting for you," he said in a clear, deep voice.

"Are you Lord Akum?" Maribel was nervously curious.

He nodded with a smile. He looked at Maribel as if he knew everything about her. The girl could not even guess the age of that personage. *He seemed eternal.*

"I brought you this," she said, offering him the bouquet she had picked up along the way.

Akum received the flowers with a smile. It seemed to Maribel that *she had known him all along.*

"My brave little girl," he said, beckoning her to sit on the surface of a boulder, from which emanated the smell of sandalwood. Akum sat and placed the flowers beside him.

"Nights are part of the days. Dreams are part of life. In them, you will find many answers to the questions that arise when you are awake."

"I often forget my dreams," Maribel admitted.

"It is not convenient to remember everything. It's best for kids to learn to listen first."

"Can I touch you?" she asked timidly. *She wanted to make sure she wasn't dreaming.* He held out his hand to her. It was warm, strong, and at the same time smooth and delicate.

"Can you fly, Lord Akum? Can you make yourself invisible? Do you know how to do magic?"

"Maybe you really want to know if it's possible to possess those skills."

Sitting on the boulder, enveloped in the fragrance of incense, Akum told Maribel the story of how he, a *Muisca* warrior, had become a sorcerer to prevent his race from being exterminated by the invaders. However, not even the power of the gods had managed to overcome the madness of the enemy. Together with a few survivors, Akum had buried much of the visible cultural heritage that drove the conquerors to destroy. He had been chosen as one of the guardians of the *Muisca* treasure. His spirit would not rest until his people were freed from oppression.

"But, more important than the treasure, it was to guard the spirit that animated our race. A spirit that marches to the rhythm of nature, makes it its friend, and does not try to subjugate it. We understood that we were in this world as creatures and not as masters. The same spirit that animated this race animates you and many children like you. You listen to the voice of your ancestors. A voice that has been silenced by centuries of ignorance and ambition. Have you heard of Yodin?"

"Yes! The Keeper of the Books." She hadn't forgotten.

"Your need to learn is guided by a special talent. That's why we have to prepare you."

"Prepare me?"

"Talent is a double-edged sword. Everything you learn must be guided by honesty and the love of truth. Your duty is to follow that route. It is a requirement if you are to fulfill your mission."

"My mission?" repeated a very confused Maribel.

"On the day of your First Communion, a double ceremony will take place. That is the day we have chosen for your initiation."

"Initia...tion?" The very word overwhelmed her.

"There is nothing to fear. You are going to be initiated into the Fellowship of the White Feather. On that day, you will know your mission."

Before Akum was done with his instructions, Maribel heard her name insistently.

"*M'hija!* Wake up!" her mother called.

Maribel found herself lying on the floor of the balcony.

***

When Maribel received the host from the hands of the Franciscan priest, her joy reflected brightly on the paten.

When she joined the other communicants on the pew, her imagination transported her back to the place where Agmmandiel waited for her. Together they flew over the river, following its course. The natural early light bathed the way with the incandescence of visions, revealing cliffs and ridges of magical rocky textures and prairies of fabulous greens and faraway blues. After a while, the girl and her guardian arrived at an emerald green forest.

Maribel could feel the refreshing spray coming from a nearby lake bordered by shrubs, trees, and herbs. All kinds of creatures of the wilderness came to greet them. Waiting in a clearing, she saw a group of people dressed in a variety of attire. Among them were Chichigua, Longtooth, and the Chinese man with the geese.

Out of a cave, Akum appeared, wearing simple warrior attire. As he walked, his movements were preceded by melodies of the forest, the jungle, and the natural kingdoms. Somehow, this otherworldly music suggested to Maribel the sacred stories of the seven races.

The *Chibcha* warrior invited Maribel to sit on the beautifully patterned blanket of red, yellow, and blue geometrical designs that he had spread on the green grass. A number of children showed up from all sides, bringing flowers and aromatic herbs. They threw petals at the warrior and the girl, then they burned the herbs inside a clay pot.

An old indigenous woman handed Agmmandiel a crystal skull, which he, in turn, brought to Akum. Then, approaching Maribel, the boy hung on her neck a pendant made out of three leaves, one of gold, another of silver, and the third of copper.

After a ceremony performed by the old woman and the children, they were offered a refreshing drink in a wooden cup that reminded the girl of Mamita's specialty: *lulo* juice.

"Look carefully," Akum said then, showing her the skull.

Maribel could see a flash of light and then what appeared to her as a blue marble ball in its center. The image quickly expanded. She saw up close, in its surface, the oceans, continents, islands, and mountains that she had seen sketched on the *Atlas* globe in her geography class. She recognized the planet. The same world that she shared with countless other beings of different sizes and colors.

People who spoke different languages and played different games. Then she saw the church, the priest, her sister, her family, her face, and her own dreams.

Akum, the chief, the teacher, the architect, the guardian of the jungles, looked into her eyes.

"Your life mission is to teach others to respect nature. Starting today, you will celebrate annually what you have seen here. On this date, every year, in solitude and communion with nature, you will write down your accomplishments. It will help you realize your ultimate goal."

"Welcome to the Fellowship," Akum said, handing Maribel a beautiful white pen that had been specially crafted in Yodin's workshops.

***

The lights of dawn through a thousand colored glasses told her the story of the saints traced by the hands of consecrated artists. Kneeling, she felt a warmth enveloping her heart. When she saw the pigeon fly towards the dome of the church, she thought of the Holy Ghost, whose grace and wisdom were to inspire her for the rest of her life.

A group of children, including Papito and Little Lucy, followed her and Miriam in admiration, wishing one day to be in their place. Their parents and grandmother, feeling proud, believed their girls were the most beautiful communicants.

Nostalgic for their own childhood, they recognized in its beauty and purity that—although most briefly—they had once had heaven on their side.

XI

Harvest Time

*Don't you know that everyone has a
Fairy World in each one?*

— P.L. Travers, Mary Poppins

The time had come to pick the maize that
Maribel and her *abuela* had sown in the lower patio.
The kernels came out in shades of yellow: golden,
pale, and whitish. They had a rich and delicate
smell. She loved, especially, the silky reddish hair
that peeked out from among the green and toasted
leaves that enveloped the cobs.

"What's that on your neck?" Mamita asked her,
looking at the primitive but beautiful necklace.

"It was among my gifts for communion
day," Maribel explained. It was the three leaves
Agmmandiel had given to her during her initiation
in the Fellowship.

"It's pretty, but it is worth a golden chain," Mamita said.

"I like it better this way."

To celebrate the harvest, Herminia and Mamita cooked corn cakes and sent the girls delivering samples to their friends.

"When is the new baby arriving?" The grocer's wife asked them.

"Soon!" the girls replied enthusiastically.

"Are you going to pass the grade?" Julieta's mom asked.

"I don't know," Maribel answered. She had paid attention, she had behaved, she had gotten good grades, she had tried her best. Still, she wasn't sure. She had spent her time speculating with her friends about the final chapter of Chan Li Po's *radionovela*. It had become fashionable among the schoolgirls to imitate the accent of the Chinese detective. There were competitions to see who could do it better.

"I think Chan should forgive her and hire her as a servant." They laughed at Amanda's wit.

"Better for her to die; no one wants her," Adalgiza sentenced.

"Let her rot in prison. She's so evil!" Mariela decided.

"And what do you think, Maribel?" They were all curious.

"She is not to be trusted. Yet, she could help the detective solve some cases."

"Bad people never change," Mariela refused to give the witch a chance.

"People like that take advantage of the kindness of others," Adalgiza replied.

"That's true. Sometimes they pretend to be good in order to deceive you. That's what my father did!" Berta knew more precisely.

***

Herminia was indisposed, so she retired to bed early. She announced that the baby was on the way. Curious and worried, they all saw their father arrive with Dr. González and a nurse. The kids were instructed by Mamita to go to her house and wait there until further notice.

"What's happening?" Little Lucy asked, intrigued.

"Well, they're going to welcome the baby," Miriam replied.

"But it is time for Chan Li Po!" complained Papito.

"Mamita just told me her radio isn't working!" exclaimed a disappointed Maribel.

"We can bring our radio here!" suggested the boy.

"Our radio is too big to bring here," said Miriam.

"Besides, we are not allowed to cross the door," Maribel reminded them.

The four kids elucidated for a while how to solve the problem. They had to find out the outcome of *The Green House* and how Chan Li Po would capture the evildoers, among them the evil witch, who had kept them on tenterhooks for so many days, doing and undoing with impunity.

Miriam and Maribel tried to get the old radio to work, without any success.

"What's wrong with the stork? Why is it taking her so long?" They asked Mamita, as she came to inspect from time to time, very nervously and excited, to assure them that everything was going well.

"The stork is on its way," she told them, and not to forget to take care of her younger sister, who by this time had fallen sound asleep in Mamita's room.

"But, it's almost nine o'clock," they complained, "the novel is about to begin!"

"Don't be selfish, my children. The novel can wait, and you can stop listening to it for a day."

"It's the final chapter, Granny!" Miriam was about to cry.

They would have to find out another way.

In a moment of silence, when all ideas were exhausted and hopes about to be lost, the unmistakable theme of the novel was heard, coming from somewhere. It didn't take long for the children to identify the source of the sound:

"It's coming from the floor!" Maribel noticed.

"The neighbors on the ground floor are listening to the novel!" Miriam pointed out.

As if their guardian angels had taken pity, the children were able to hear the radio through the cracks when they pressed their ears on the wooden floor.

"I can barely hear!" Miriam complained.

"Chan Li Po already knows who the bad guys are and where they are hiding," Maribel interpreted.

"Raise the volume on the radio!" Papito shouted through the cracks.

For a moment, the radio waves disappeared, and a man's sullen voice came out of the cracks:

"Get off there, or I'm complaining to your dad!"

"He turned the volume off!" Maribel said desperately.

"And now what do we do?" Miriam asked, on the verge of tears.

"We'll have to wait until tomorrow for our schoolmates to tell us."

The spitting image of disappointment and frustration was scattered around the room.

It wasn't long before the door, which connected the houses, opened. Mamita appeared sweaty but jubilant, as if she had run a marathon to bring them the news.

"Come and see your little brother!" she announced.

Burdened with the hope that they would have enough time, all three children rushed through the door. Maribel, who arrived first, turned on the radio, tuned in to the station, and sat down with her siblings to listen to how Chan Li Po confronted the witch.

"He caught her!" Miriam shouted, full of joy.

Sitting on the floor, before the incredulous gaze of the adults, the children heard the Chinese detective pronounce with his peculiar accent: "He who goes badly, ends badly," and they completely agreed. Certain that the witch would spend the rest of her days in prison, they listened to the theme song, closing the final chapter of the novel.

Excited, they got up to meet the newborn child. And while the announcer read the names of the cast, Papito suggested to his mother that they please baptize his little brother with the name of Chan Li Po.

XII

The Final Act

*A*mong the many things she had learned at the Boyacá school was that the Final Act was the program prepared by the teachers with the participation of the students, to show parents the talents of their daughters. It was in this way that they discovered the wonderful voice of Gabriela Valencia and Maribel's unsuspected genius for memorizing poems. The entertainment was, of course, a prelude to recognizing the merit of students and their effort during the nine months that the school year lasted.

The event had a dual purpose, however: As the parents relaxed, the delivery of the report card was left for the very end. After that, there were no more opportunities to complain or to defend oneself. Nothing more to say. The ruling was final.

Maribel wasn't entirely sure she had saved the year in the final exams. In spite of everything, *she had already tested her faith by asking in writing and with the help of the white pen, that they would please save her from failure.* Agmmandiel had told her in her latest encounter that she could expect miracles, but that didn't mean that bitter surprises wouldn't come. *Maybe she had failed one of the subjects she liked the least. Or maybe she should repeat the whole year. It was like dying to be born again.*

"Are you going to pass this year?" Half the world had asked her during the course of that day. Not even she herself knew the answer.

Hoping to calm down, she had accepted the invitation to play the spit game with her friends. It had been Berta Castillo who had introduced them to the magic of this rite: make a circle with the tip of the thumb attached to the tip of the index finger, measure the distance from the head to the ground, and spit to get the saliva to pass cleanly through the narrow circle. If it goes through neatly, the answer is yes. If not, well, sometimes it failed, but there were always two other chances.

Maribel felt that the only thing that restored her confidence was to touch the three metallic leaves that were now hanging from her neck. She remembered to finish the request with the magic words of the language of flowers, *selam, selam,* and the fear vanished. At least for a while.

The time had come for the delivery of the diplomas. Maribel heard the names of all her friends pass by, in the categories of "award for conduct," "award for application," and "award for collaboration." Her name was not heard, and hope vanished from her mother's face.

Finally, when no one was paying attention anymore, the last prize that seemed so insignificant to everyone, and that she thought was made up so as not to leave anyone without mention: "for companionship."

Companionship! Companionship? There was commotion in the audience because people wanted to find out what exactly that meant.

It was unquestionably a consolation prize. "Your daughter is a good friend of mine," Don Arturo's serene voice informed Herminia. "The talent of companionship is rare in this world. It is very rare for a human being to learn from childhood to listen to others. It is like a bond between people."

Herminia didn't seem very convinced, but she felt proud anyway. Don Arturo, the famous healer, had taken the time to talk about her daughter.

Surprised, Maribel observed the three metal leaves hanging from Amanda's father's keychain. Instinctively, she put her hand to her neck to check with joy if hers were still there.

She walked away silently and thoughtfully.

Mariela was waiting for her at the school door to say goodbye and give her a handkerchief on which she had painted two colorful parakeets.

"Where's your mom?" Maribel asked Mariela when she noticed her absence.

"They didn't give her permission at the candle factory," the girl replied.

"My grandmom says I'm going to religious school," a very sad Adalgiza told them.

"Let me know which school you're going to, so I can ask my brother to enroll me there," Nelly said, trying to console her friend.

Berta was to return to her native town, whatever that was, taking back her talent for storytelling. Amanda couldn't speak at all. She said goodbye to Maribel and the rest of the gang with a kiss and cloudy eyes.

"We're moving to a house up north of the city. Your father has been promoted," Herminia announced to her children.

"And what about our *guaca*?" Maribel asked.

"It was just a dream, my child," she sighed, almost relieved.

Thus, Mamita and Herminia prepared a cookout to celebrate Rigoberto's promotion and the end of the school year.

The family owed gratitude to Miriam for having saved the day from a bad streak. She had been awarded a medal for conduct and a diploma of recognition for her "excellence in art." She was so elated that she had gone out to share her happiness with her friends in the neighborhood.

Papito had barely passed the grade, and he had retired to the balcony to build paper airplanes with the pages of his notebooks.

From her home's window, Maribel saw the last of the schoolgirls go home with one or two parents. She was sad she had to leave the school, the house, and the valley, where all her real and fictitious friends lived. Above all, she was nostalgic that she would have to separate from Mamita and her cat, Micifú.

The sun was turning reddish, and the afternoon was becoming night. Everything was back to normal. No more homework for two months. No more numbers or anxiety. At least until next February.

She promised herself to pay more attention and make a greater effort in the fourth grade. After all, she had to prepare for her assigned mission in life. How was she going to carry it out? She didn't know. It was a great responsibility, but she still had a lot of time ahead of her. She wanted to meet Yodin so that he could reveal to her the secrets of knowledge. Then, she would see. She was concerned, however, with the fact that, since her initiation, Agmmandiel hadn't shown up.

She saw the three teachers, Doña Lola, Doña Ana, and Miss Sofia, lock doors and windows as they exited the school. Maribel spied on them, hidden behind the curtains as they headed for the bus stop.

The girl didn't think twice. She stuck her legs out of the window. As they crossed the street, the women glanced at the strange scene: a pair of children's legs dangling out. Maribel could not hold back her laughter when *she imagined the surprise painted on her teachers' faces.*

Proudly and still smiling, Maribel went to the family desk to open the drawer where she now kept her writing tools. Lifting the lid of the box of cookies, where she kept her most precious objects, she deposited the three metal leaves and took out the white pen.

She opened the bottle and filled it with blue ink to begin writing her first story.

The End

BIOGRAPHICAL DATA OF THE AUTHOR

Gloria Chávez Vásquez is a writer, journalist and educator of Colombian origin who has lived in the United States since 1970. Her writings have appeared in Noticias del Mundo, El Diario/La prensa, Impacto, El Espectador, El Tiempo, La Crónica del Quindío, Revista Manizales, *Animal Agenda*, Revista ADDA, El Díario/La Prensa, Noticias del Mundo, Visión, Linden Lane, Legerete Magazine, El Gato Tuerto, *Ruptures*, Temas del Caribe. Letras del Parnaso, Democracia Participativa, Insularis Magazine, Zoepost, El Quindiano, Las dos orillas, Cola de Rata, as well as other publications in the United States, Canada, Mexico, Colombia, Brasil and Spain.

Published books:

Bilingual

Opus Americanus. Collection of short stories; White Owl Editions, New York, 1993

Akum, The Magic of Dreams. Novel; White Owl Editions, New York, 1996

Spanish

Mariposa Mentalis. Novel; Verbum Editions, Madrid, 2024

Yodin's Book. Novel; White Owl Editions, New York, 2016

Anthology of Short Stories. *Narrative; University of Quindío, Armenia, 2015*

Agmandiel, The Way of the Kingdoms. Novel; White Owl Editions, New York 2011

Chronicles of the Last Judgment. Collection of short stories; White Owl Editions. New York 2006

Soul Predators. Collection of short stories; White Owl Editions, New York, 2003

Cuajada, The Count of Jasmine. Novelette; *Universidad del Quindío, Armenia, 1989, Herencia Books,* New York, 1999

Akum, The Magic of Dreams. Novel; Editorial *Tercer Mundo,* Bogotá, 1983

Tales of Quindío. Collection of short stories; Editorial *Quingráficas*, Armenia, 1982

Las Termitas, Collection of stories; *Union of Colombian Writers,* 1978

See website:
www.gloriachavezvasquez.com

Gloria Chávez Vásquez

El Camino de los Reinos

Agmmandiel

Book Two of the Akum Trilogy

Agmmandiel, the Way of the Realms, tells the story of Maribel, a twelve-year-old girl, who, through her adventures during the Christmas season, transports us with her imagination to the world where the wonderful and the fantastic are mixed with reality. Maribel, as she did in *Akum, the Magic of Dreams*, must face new challenges. Turned into a detective, she must defend her reputation and free herself from the unfair suspicions that weigh on her in her family. Reality in the world around her is sometimes painful, but Agmmandiel, the indigenous elf, guides her by supporting her decisions.

Maribel attends Agmmandiel's initiation as one of the guardians of the path of the realms. More than a family story, *Agmmandiel* is a hymn to life and a guide to physical, spiritual, and intellectual growth for readers going through the early stages and preparing for life's challenges, a story rich in youth mythology, as well as local traditions and social values.

El libro de Yodín

Autora de Akum, La magia de los sueños y Agmmandiel,
El camino de los reinos

GLORIA CHÁVEZ VÁSQUEZ

Book Three of the Akum Trilogy

The book of Yodin is the third in the trilogy that began with A*kum, the Magic of Dreams* and continued with *Agmmandiel, the Way of the Realms*. Already in her early adolescence, Maribel discovers, explores, and studies the new community in which she and her family live and whose atmosphere transforms, with the days, into a heavy and chaotic culture. The society of the neighborhood and the school are a source of oppression and aggressiveness, dangerous to her increasingly independent personality. To top it off, a predator is on the loose in the city, taking advantage of the shadows to sacrifice her young victims. Her role in that narrow society is doubtful, and Maribel dreams of the quiet and harmonious place created in her imagination with the help of books where she can lead a more normal and productive social and adult life. There are only two options: the one offered by Juanita, a rebellious and dreamy girl like her, or the solution offered by her apprenticeship with Yodin, the magician sage who appears at this stage of her life.

* 9 7 9 8 9 9 9 2 3 0 5 2 2 *